"Damn it, Lisa, don't look at me like that."

"Like what?"

"Like you're as curious about me as I am about you."

"Curious?" she asked.

"If you were a few years older—"

She cut him off, angry. "And exactly what difference would a few years make? You're acting as if I don't know the score. I'm twenty-one, I can vote, drink and kiss any man I want."

His hands rested on her shoulders now. "A kiss could start something neither of us are ready for."

"Or it could prove there's nothing for either of us to worry about. You know—all smoke and no fire."

"Oh, Lisa." Her name was a protest…a warning.

She could back away now when she still had the chance.

But she didn't want to back away.

Dear Reader,

It is always an honor to take part in a continuity series. I had a special fondness for my heroine Lisa, since I created her for the original LOGAN'S LEGACY single-title series. Her Prince Charming, a Texas tycoon, gives her a Valentine's Day fantasy date that she'll remember forever.

Valentine's Day has always been special for my husband and me—we exchange hearts again, as well as presents, remembering the romance that first drew us together. It is an occasion for us to renew our commitment to each other, to celebrate our romantic journey thus far and the future we are building together.

I wish my readers a happy Valentine's Day.

All my best,

Karen Rose Smith

FALLING FOR THE TEXAS TYCOON

KAREN ROSE SMITH

Silhouette®

SPECIAL EDITION®

Published by Silhouette Books

America's Publisher of Contemporary Romance

Special thanks and acknowledgment are given
to Karen Rose Smith for her contribution to
LOGAN'S LEGACY REVISITED.

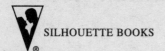 SILHOUETTE BOOKS

ISBN-13: 978-0-373-24807-0
ISBN-10:   0-373-24807-5

FALLING FOR THE TEXAS TYCOON

Books by Karen Rose Smith

Silhouette Special Edition

Abigail and Mistletoe #930
The Sheriff's Proposal #1074
His Little Girl's Laughter #1426
Expecting the CEO's Baby #1535
Their Baby Bond #1588
Take a Chance on Me #1599
Which Child Is Mine? #1655
Cabin Fever #1682
Custody for Two #1753
The Baby Trail #1767
Expecting His Brother's Baby #1779
The Super Mom #1797
Falling for the Texas Tycoon #1807

*Baby Bonds

Silhouette Books

The Fortunes of Texas
Marry in Haste...

Logan's Legacy
A Precious Gift

The Fortunes of Texas: Reunion
The Good Doctor

Signature Select

Secret Admirer
"Dream Marriage"

KAREN ROSE SMITH

Karen Rose Smith, award-winning author of over fifty published novels, loves to write. She began putting pen to paper in high school when she discovered poetry as a creative outlet. Also writing for her high school newspaper, intending to teach someday, she never suspected crafting emotional and romantic stories would become her life's work! Married for thirty-five years, she and her husband reside in Pennsylvania with their two cats, Ebbie and London. Readers can e-mail Karen through her Web site at www.karenrosesmith.com or write to her at P. O. Box 1545, Hanover, PA 17331.

To my husband, Steve. Happy Valentine's Day!

Chapter One

Men like Alan Barrett were trouble with a capital T. With his Stetson and his I-can-beat-down-any-obstacle-in-my-path smile, he obviously thought he could get his own way no matter what.

He was *wrong*.

Although Lisa Sanders had been her boss's gatekeeper for only a month, she was already good at it. No one charmed or intimidated her. Not even a six-foot-two Texan who claimed to be a friend of Brian's. He was not listed on her boss's schedule and that's all that mattered.

She stared into his to-die-for blue eyes, ignored the runaway beat of her pulse and repeated, "Mr. Summers is in a meeting and can't be disturbed. His schedule is tight today. I might be able to fit you in around one-fifteen."

Alan Barrett's smile faded. "Look, Miss—" His gaze dropped to the nameplate on her desk. "Miss Sanders. Besides the fact that we do business together, Brian and I are friends. I spoke to him less than an hour ago. He said he'd meet with me at ten. It's now ten."

Lisa wasn't simply fresh out of college with a degree in business, she had a history of street smarts behind her, one that made her square her shoulders and act even more protective of Brian. He wasn't only her boss. He and his wife, Carrie, were her benefactors. If it weren't for them, she didn't know where she'd be now. Maybe still in a homeless shelter, her baby put up for adoption to people she didn't know. Brian and Carrie had given her a home and a new life, and she would be forever grateful to them. As soon as she earned her real estate license, she'd be more than Brian's office manager, and she'd never *ever* let him down. She wanted him to know he could depend on her just as she'd depended on him.

Motioning to the group of pale gray, leather-covered club chairs in the waiting area where the receptionist was located—Alan Barrett had bypassed the admin and come straight to her—Lisa said firmly but politely, "If you take a seat, I'll check with Mr. Summers when his meeting is over."

The Texan's gaze became steely as he assessed everything from Lisa's chin-length bob and navy suit to her color of lipstick. A slight shiver trembled through her when she realized she was attracted to his raw sex appeal, the jut of his rugged jaw, his broad, muscular shoulders.

Even with his hat shadowing his face, the lines there told her he had to be near forty. He was way too old for her and definitely out of her league. She didn't react to men this way. She had no time for men. She was on a career path. Besides all that, she doubted she could find a man who could accept the fact that she'd given away her child.

"Since I haven't seen you here before, Miss Sanders, I'll take into consideration the fact that you're probably new and trying to do a good job. But if you don't buzz Brian and let him know I'm here, you might lose it."

She'd suspected this man might try to turn to intimidation tactics. His type always did. She didn't do well with patronizing authority figures. The other employees who worked for Brian were under the illusion that she was a relative of her boss's and he'd given her this job to help her get a good start. Only his and Carrie's closest friends knew the whole story—that they'd taken her in in her eighth month of pregnancy, when she was eighteen, had adopted her baby and treated her like a daughter ever since, including paying for her college tuition. If Mr. Barrett didn't "know" about her, then how close a friend of Brian's could he be?

"Believe me, Mr. Barrett, I'm not going to lose my job. If you don't want to have a seat, then I guess you'll have to leave."

If Alan Barrett was surprised she hadn't backed down, he hid it well. Glancing at his watch again, he said in an I'm-not-happy-about-this-but-I'll-deal-with-it voice, "I needed to see Brian immediately because I have an important call to make in half an hour. Do you have a conference room I can use so I can make it now?"

She'd rarely known men like Alan Barrett to be flexible. She supposed Brian wouldn't mind if he used one of the offices. She'd just have to keep an eye on him. Pushing back the contract she'd been studying, she stood.

"Follow me," she said crisply, then led him to a hall to the right of her desk. The hairs at the nape of her neck prickled as he followed her. She hoped her suit jacket wasn't wrinkled yet. She hoped the back seam of her skirt was straight. She hoped...

She hoped *nothing* where this man was concerned. When his business with Brian was finished, he'd be gone.

At the first conference room they reached, she opened the door and let it swing inward. Not intending to enter, she started to move out of the way. But she wasn't quite quick enough. As she turned to sidestep, there was Alan Barrett practically nose to nose with her. Or more like nose to chest.

When she looked up, her breath caught in her throat. She inhaled his cologne, which was woodsy and male, and felt so small and fragile standing near him it was as if he could swallow her up. The fabric of his Western-cut suit coat brushed her own jacket. There was a flicker in his eyes, a tightening of his lips. Did that mean *he* was affected, too?

What was happening that she was having fantasies at work? Maybe she should take Carrie's advice and go out on a few dates, even if she didn't intend to get serious with anyone.

Regrouping, she quickly stepped away from him. "Take as long as you like. When Brian finishes with his meeting, I'll tell him you're here."

Then, feeling as if she were running from the devil himself, she hurried back to the safety of her desk and the work that was going to be her future.

Alan didn't like to be kept waiting.

He never sat on the sidelines—not at the family ranch in Texas, not when he was working in real estate wherever it took him. For the past year, he'd been dividing his time between Texas and Portland, Oregon, doing more deals with Brian here and in other areas of the West Coast.

Unable to help himself, he looked out at the blond-haired young woman who had barred him from Brian's door. Damn, he was used to getting his own way, and he wasn't accustomed to his pulse racing as it had when he'd looked into her green eyes and heart-shaped face. With a low oath, he told himself Lisa Sanders was probably not much older than his daughter.

Turning away from her with some reluctance—and wondering if she was as efficient as she looked—he went over to the window and peered down the five stories. Taking his phone from his belt, he dialed his daughter's school. This call to Christina's guidance counselor was important. She'd been accepted at Stanford and USC, though she was seriously considering the University of Illinois because of the animal sciences program. His ex-wife didn't like that idea at all. She wanted Christina to pursue psychology or premed, a more highbrow science. But his daughter had her own mind. She was the light of his life and, to his consternation, could usually get him to side with her. Sherri would also be having this discussion about colleges with Christina's guidance counselor either today or tomorrow.

Alan brought up the guidance counselor's name and pressed Send. Hopefully, she'd be free and they could have their discussion a little bit early.

Half an hour later, finished with his conversation, he exited the conference room. About to approach Lisa Sanders and demand again she tell Brian he was here, he stopped to watch her a moment as she opened mail. Her bob was chic and blunt-cut, swinging forward when she tilted her head. Her suit fit her slim body as if it was custom-made. Her white blouse had a demure scoop neck, and he saw she was wearing a locket. A present from a boyfriend?

Probably.

Alarm bells went off and he told himself not to even wonder about it. He'd never had a penchant for younger women, so why start now?

But there had been a maturity in Lisa Sanders's eyes when she looked at him that had almost startled him.

Now she quickly slit open an envelope, took out the sheet of paper...and went absolutely white.

What kind of mail could cause *that* reaction?

As he approached her, he saw her hands were shaking. "What's wrong?" he asked, standing in front of her desk.

She was still staring at the sheet of paper in her hand.

"Miss Sanders, are you all right?"

The sound of her name must have caught her attention, and she glanced up. When their gazes met, he felt that full-body impact again. He looked deeper and thought he saw fear. What was this young woman afraid of?

Putting on her official office manager's face again, she blinked, took a deep breath, then replied, "I'm fine."

"Your hands are trembling."

She looked down at them, then at the letter. Folding it, she quickly tucked it into her suit jacket. "I'm just a little…cold, I guess, with the damp weather outside and all…."

When he was in Portland it seemed as if it was always damp. But he could sense a lie when he heard it, and she was lying through her teeth. She wasn't cold. She was upset about that letter in her pocket.

It was none of his business.

Since his encounter with Brian's gatekeeper earlier, he hadn't pegged her for a shrinking violet. The letter she'd received in the mail must have upset her greatly.

Suddenly men's voices burst from behind the closed door. Seconds later, Brian and two men Alan assumed were clients were standing near Lisa's desk. Brian greeted Alan and introduced him to the men, who soon excused themselves and left Summers Development. All the while, Alan kept one eye on Lisa, who was still pale and fidgeting with messages that had probably come in while Brian was in his meeting.

After the clients left, Brian turned to Alan. "It's good to see you again. I missed you this past month. How are things in Texas?"

"My brother's a good manager. I don't have to worry when I'm away from the ranch."

Now Brian turned to Lisa to include her in the conversation. "I guess you've met Mr. Barrett?"

Lisa gave her boss what Alan suspected was a forced smile. "Yes, I have. I didn't want to interrupt you when he arrived," she admitted honestly.

"Alan and I've been doing a lot of work together. You can always interrupt me when he shows up." Brian took the messages she handed to him, flipped through them, then stuffed them into his pocket. "I'll take care of these later. I want to get our meeting started. Lisa, I'd like you to sit in."

Her green eyes went wide with surprise. "You would?"

"Sure," Brian said easily. "The only way you're going to get experience is to be involved in what I do. When you earn your real estate license, you'll really be ready to go. You might want to take some notes for us, too."

Ever since Alan had stood within three feet of Lisa, he could smell her perfume. It was a haunting fragrance, somewhere between flowers and musk. Now he got another good whiff as she leaned toward her desk, grabbing a notepad and pen.

Stepping aside, he motioned for her to precede him into Brian's office. Their gazes held for just a second too long and he felt that jolt of adrenaline again that had been missing from his life for many years.

As Alan waited for Lisa to be seated in one of the chairs in front of Brian's desk, Brian explained, "Lisa graduated in December with a degree in business."

"Margery left?" Fifty-five years old now, Margery had been Brian's office manager for as long as Alan had been working with him.

"Margery's husband retired and she's traveling with him. Lisa's only taking over the job temporarily until she has her license."

Alan wondered why Brian had chosen Lisa out of all the people he could have hired for the position. Why would he be waiting for her to earn her license to join his team? Why wouldn't he hire someone with experience?

As he checked out Brian's interaction with Lisa, he didn't see any evidence that his colleague was enamored with the young woman, or that Lisa was attracted to Brian. Still, one never knew what went on behind closed doors. Brian had once alluded to a rocky time in his marriage, but Allan had never seen evidence of that, and with adopting Timothy, he and Carrie seemed to have absolutely everything they wanted.

Studying Lisa, Alan thought she still looked unsettled. She was staring down at her pad, pen in hand, ready to take notes. But he sensed she was distracted.

He was sure of it when Brian began talking about the project they were working on. She was writing, but not much, and she didn't look up.

"I got the paperwork you faxed me yesterday," Brian

said to Alan. "All of the properties look as if they'll be suitable. Do you have a meeting set up with the investors?"

"Next Thursday. I thought we could fly down on Wednesday. Does that fit your schedule?"

"That should work out fine. Lisa, I'm going to want you to fly along on this trip and be an assistant to both me and Alan."

When his office manager didn't look up, Brian said a little more loudly, "Lisa?"

Her head came up then and she flushed, putting color back into her cheeks. "I'm sorry. What did you say?"

Brian's brows quirked up. "I said I want you to fly to Texas with me and Alan and act as our assistant on this venture. I hope we can put together a deal for the golf resort. Fortunately, it's practically in Alan's backyard and we're going to be staying at his family's ranch."

"You're sure you want me to come along?" She glanced at Alan, as if being in close proximity to him wasn't a good idea.

He didn't know whether to be insulted or flattered.

"No better way to get your feet wet," Brian assured her.

"I'm still furnishing my apartment and—"

"As long as you have a bed to sleep in and a chair to sit on, that can wait, can't it?" her boss asked.

Again Lisa glanced at Alan. "Of course it can. I guess I'm just anxious to settle into my own place."

"You know Carrie and I will help you do that any way we can, including shoving around furniture."

As the discussion turned back to business, Lisa took

copious notes, as if she'd put her distraction behind her. This young woman intrigued Alan, and he'd known her less than a morning.

After the discussion about the proposed golf resort wound down, he checked his watch. "I'd better be going. I have another meeting in half an hour and then I'll see you again at four to discuss the Sacramento resort with Joe Dulchek."

When Brian stood with a nod, Alan and Lisa rose, too, and found themselves standing very close together. He was a good six inches taller than she was. She was so slim and fragile-looking, yet the set of her shoulders and the fire in her eyes told him she'd fight for whatever she wanted. The term spitfire came to mind. Her perfume tempted him again, and he found himself studying her face.

He wasn't sure what prodded him to say it, but before she went her way and he went his, he advised her, "Bring comfortable clothes along to Texas when you pack. If you have boots, throw those in, too. We've got horses if you want to ride."

She said softly, "I've only been riding once before."

"We've got a few gentle horses."

"He's being modest," Brian interjected. "They breed cutting horses as well as their own cattle. You school them, too, don't you?"

"When I have the time. Neal does most of that now. I've been away from the ranch so much this past year, he's taken on horses I know nothing about."

Lisa looked at her boss again. "How long will we be staying at Mr. Barrett's?"

"We'll probably be there three or four days. We'll see how the meetings progress and how much property we can get covered."

"Should I make airline reservations?"

"No need for that. I've got my own jet," Alan explained. "My pilot can be ready at a hour's notice if he has to be."

When Alan mentioned his jet, most women looked impressed, but not Lisa Sanders. She simply said, "I see."

"If you have those notes on my desk by the end of the day, that will be fine," Brian informed her. Then he asked, "You're going to lunch with Craig, aren't you?"

She nodded and her lips turned up in a genuine smile. "I have to get changed. No way do I want to ride on his bike dressed like this." She held out her hand to Alan. "It's good to meet you, Mr. Barrett. Next time you come in, I'll make sure to buzz Brian right away."

Was she mending fences because they were going to be working together? Taking her hand, he realized it was cool to the touch—at first. Her handshake seemed to generate heat that flowed through him like aged bourbon.

They released each other at the same time, and he thought she looked as startled as he felt. Damn, this was a kind of chemistry he'd never had with a woman before. How was that even possible? At thirty-eight, hadn't he had every kind of experience there was with women?

Looking a bit flustered, Lisa left Brian's office.

Brian was shuffling through a few papers on his desk when Alan asked, "How old is she?"

"Lisa? She's twenty-one."

"Are you sure you don't want someone more experienced to sit in on these meetings? I can have someone join us from my office in Rocky Ridge."

"Lisa's young, but she's a hard worker and she learns fast. She went through four years of college in three and a half, even with working summers. Still, if you'd feel more confident having one of your people involved…"

Alan had never had any reason to doubt Brian's judgment. "No, if you feel she's what we need, that's fine."

As he left Brian's office a short time later, after a discussion about the colleges Christina was considering, he stopped short. A young man who appeared to be about Lisa's age was escorting her through the double glass doors. He looked like a biker with his shaggy hair, leather jacket, pierced brow, earrings and boots. Then Alan noticed Lisa. She'd changed, all right—into a long-sleeved black sweater that molded to her breasts and hugged her waist, and low-slung black jeans with a belt studded with rhinestones. She also carried a leather jacket over one arm, and her boots were similar to the young man's.

Seeing the two of them together made Alan feel every one of his thirty-eight years. In spite of that, he acknowledged what he'd felt that morning when Lisa Sanders had barred his way and stood up to him. He'd had the overwhelming urge to kiss her.

If that wasn't an insane fantasy, he didn't know what

was. But he was not going to let his imagination take on a life of its own. He was not going to think about Lisa Sanders again, except as Brian's office manager who would be assisting them on this project.

End of story.

After locking the door to the unisex bathroom at Summers Development, Lisa pulled her sweater over her head so she could change back into her business suit. The upside-down mermaid tattoo on her left arm practically winked at her. The peace sign tattoo high on her other wrist also reminded her she was trying to leave her past behind. No one here knew about her tattoos except Brian, of course. She always kept them covered. They really weren't befitting an up-and-coming professional.

As if it were calling to her again, she reached for the note in her jeans pocket. Opening it, she read, *"You owe me. Don't think I've forgotten."*

Closing her eyes, she took a deep breath. She'd almost told Craig about it. After all, they'd been friends when she'd returned to Portland, pregnant. Back then, after she'd had Timothy, she'd even thought they might connect romantically. But they never really had. Craig was two years older than she was, protective and they'd settled into a friendship that was valuable and she hoped lasting.

The note looked as if it had been generated by computer on plain white paper. When she was homeless and living on the streets, she'd met some shady characters. She'd met pimps who wanted her to turn tricks for them. She'd met drug dealers and avoided them, but not before they checked her over, trying to figure what she could do for them.

And then there was Thad, Timothy's biological father. He'd wanted nothing to do with her and the baby because he'd had his own plans. How could the note be from him, when he'd signed away his parental rights?

Just as she had.

The difference was, she was still connected to Timothy and always would be. Some nights her heart ached unbearably because of the decision she'd made. But she'd known it was best for Timothy then, and she believed it was best for him now.

What did this note mean, anyway? Was it a precursor to blackmail? Did someone think that, since she was connected to Brian and Carrie, *she* had money, too?

Folding the note, she slipped it into her purse. She'd have to think about it some more before she told anyone. Besides, what was there to tell? She was certainly not going to worry Brian and Carrie unnecessarily, not after everything they'd done for her. She was making a life on her own now and she wouldn't depend on anyone else.

The locket around her neck swung free as she bent to remove her boots and then her jeans. In only her panties and bra, she opened the heart necklace and looked at the little face of the baby she'd given away, touched the silky lock of his hair.

"You're happy where you are," she said, her voice

catching. "That's all that matters. Carrie and Brian love you as if you were their very own."

Standing up straight and squaring her shoulders, she quickly dressed in her suit and high heels, ran a comb through her hair, reapplied lipstick and gazed at the professional woman she was trying to become.

Alan Barrett's tanned face with its firm jaw and crooked lines around his eyes seemed to gaze back at her. She blinked. Alan was years older than she was. He was Brian's colleague. He was too handsome and he knew it. He was a little bit arrogant, determined and even authoritarian.

So why couldn't she stop thinking about him?

Because he'd looked at her with such concern after she'd opened the note? Or because when their eyes met, she felt rattled down to her spike heels?

She doubted very much if Alan Barrett would like a woman with tattoos.

She doubted if Alan Barrett would even consider getting involved with a woman who had given up her child.

Chapter Two

During a game of hide-and-seek that evening, Lisa spotted Timothy by the leg of the dining room table. "I see you!"

Giggling, he dashed under the table, where the white cloth partially hid him. After she crouched down, Lisa got to her hands and knees and went after him. As she caught him, he laughed.

"You can't hide from me," she warned him, tickling his tummy.

When Carrie spoke, Lisa could hardly hear her above their laughter. Releasing Timothy, she peered out from under the tablecloth.

Carrie was smiling, and she wasn't alone. "Brian brought a friend home for dinner."

As Lisa's gaze traveled from boots, up expensive

slacks to the Western-cut jacket, she practically groaned. The friend that Brian had brought home was Alan Barrett.

Minus his Stetson, he looked amused as he said, "I used to do that with my daughter. In some ways, it seems as if it were yesterday."

Carrie explained, "Alan's daughter will be leaving for college in the fall."

He had a daughter. He was married. Lisa almost breathed a sigh of relief at that news.

Timothy chose that moment to scramble away from her and run to his mom, snagging Carrie by one leg. "Can I have a cookie, please?"

A beautiful woman and a former model, Carrie stooped and lifted Timothy into her arms. Her auburn hair hid her face until she absently brushed it away. "It's almost bedtime. I suppose you can have a cookie if you have a glass of milk with it."

One of those little pangs stabbed Lisa's heart. Carrie had final say in everything Timothy did. She was a wonderful mom and Lisa couldn't have found anyone better to be a mother to her son.

Crawling out from under the table, Lisa felt foolish. When she'd arrived at Carrie and Brian's, she'd changed from her suit into the clothes she had worn to have lunch with Craig. Now she was rumpled after roughhousing with Timothy. She knew her hair was probably a mess and her lipstick nonexistent. Some professional image she was projecting to a man she'd be working with!

Ruffling Timothy's hair, Brian said, "I'm going to

check messages in my office." After loosening his tie, he motioned to the top of the buffet and suggested to Alan, "Make yourself at home. Drinks are there. Lisa can tell you where anything is if you can't find it."

"Dinner will be ready as soon as I get this little rascal a snack and put him to bed," Carrie added. "I'm so glad you could join us, Alan. Please do make yourself at home."

A few moments later, the dining room seemed small and quiet with just the two of them in it. Alan seemed to tower over Lisa. Awkward tension vibrated between them until he stepped toward the buffet.

Searching for some topic of conversation, Lisa asked, "Where will your daughter be going to school?"

Alan picked up an old-fashioned glass and tipped the lid from the ice bucket. "She has to make up her mind soon. I'll find out when I get back to the ranch next week."

"I imagine it's hard to be away from your family when you travel for work."

Although Lisa had told herself from the moment of Timothy's birth that he was no longer hers, although she'd given him to Brian and Carrie so he'd have a secure future where hers had been uncertain, she'd still missed him terribly when she'd gone off to college. She'd thought once she'd started her own life she could put her past behind her and move on. That had included reconciling herself to the fact that although she'd given birth to a son, he was no longer hers and she was not a mother. But even her heavy load of course work hadn't been able to make her forget about Timothy, though her resolve had always been strong and sure. She had done what was best for him. Thankful that Brian and Carrie were letting her stay involved in his life, she knew that the dull ache in her heart might never go away. But she'd always be a backup to Brian and Carrie. She just hoped as Timothy matured and learned the truth, he'd understand. Most of all, she hoped that he'd forgive her.

"I *have* been away a lot the past six months," Alan replied. "Most of the time I've been working up here in Portland with Brian. I bought a condo in the fall to cut back on hotel bills." He flashed the crooked grin that made Lisa's toes curl in her boots.

He's married, she scolded herself. No toe-curling allowed.

"Did I hear you say you got a new apartment?" he asked, glancing at her.

Alan had apparently been in and out of Brian's life for the past six months, but she didn't know what Brian might have told him. So she treaded carefully.

"Yes, I'm furnishing it, little by little. I dropped over tonight because Carrie had some extra things in the attic she thought I could use."

"Brian and Carrie are a great couple. Truth be told, I never thought I'd want a partner, but Brian's got great instincts and something else that's hard to find these days—integrity." He poured Scotch into his glass and then soda. "Can I fix you something?" he asked when he was done.

That surprised her, and he must have seen it in her expression.

"What? You think a man can't fix a drink for a lady? Believe me, whenever Christina stays with me, I hear about the changing roles of men and women. I think she even did a paper on it."

"Stays with you?" That sounded as if—

"Yes. I've had joint custody with my ex-wife since Christina was ten."

"You're...divorced?"

"Yes, I am."

The toe-curling was back double-time now. "Maybe I will have a club soda," she murmured.

"Ice?" he asked.

She nodded, then watched as his very large, tanned hands took the tongs and dropped three cubes into the glass. After he unscrewed the lid, he poured in the soda. He and Lisa reached for a lime slice at the same time. His fingers were hot, and when her skin touched his, she became hot, too. She knew a flush rose to her cheeks as she pulled back and let him add the fruit to her glass. When he handed it to her, she was careful that their fingers didn't meet.

"Your lunch date looked like an interesting guy," Alan remarked nonchalantly.

"Craig and I have known each other since..." She stopped. "For a long time."

"You dated through college?"

"No. We kept in touch, but with him in Portland and me at college, we went our separate ways."

"But now you're back and he's here, too."

Was Alan fishing or just making conversation? She had the feeling he was going to cast out a few more lines, and she didn't want to answer his questions. They were going to be working together, and she didn't want him to be judging her while they were. And he *would* judge her if he found out about Timothy. She was sure of it. She did *not* want Brian's friend looking at her as the homeless, unwed mother she'd once been. Maybe it was pride on her part, but she was trying to create a future.

"I'm going to see if Timothy finished his snack. Maybe I can read him a bedtime story before dinner. If you'll excuse me…"

After a long, studying look, Alan tipped his glass to her. "Bedtime stories are almost as important as good-night kisses. Enjoy."

His words lingered as she went to the kitchen to find Timothy. Alan sounded as if he understood. He sounded as if he knew the importance of being a father.

One more reason to keep her past a secret.

During dinner, Alan's gaze kept going back to Lisa again and again, in spite of his intentions to have a pleasant meal with Brian and Carrie and ignore the young woman who'd been in and out of his thoughts all afternoon. Damn it, she had a pretty face. Yes, she had glossy hair he'd love to run his hands through. Yes, she had a curvy figure that looked wonderful in low-slung jeans. And those boots—

He stabbed a bite of cake as if it might run away from

him. He wanted a few questions answered. He and Brian
weren't close friends—not yet, anyway—but he'd been
here for dinner before and there had never been any talk
about Lisa Sanders. Yet here she was, acting as if she was
a relative of some kind.

"So, Lisa, have you always lived in Portland?"

After a quick glance at Brian, she wiped her mouth
with her napkin and seemed to consider an answer carefully. Finally she revealed, "I lived in Seattle with an aunt
for a couple of years. But I was born in Portland and I
always considered it my home."

"She's a friend of the family," Carrie added casually.
"We watch out for her."

So they *weren't* related. "You're very good with
Timothy," Alan remarked. "I thought maybe Carrie
had hired you to help out so you could earn extra
money for college."

The two women exchanged a look.

"I help out because we're friends," Lisa answered
quietly.

There was an uncomfortable silence that Alan didn't
understand. Then Carrie focused her attention on Lisa.
"Speaking of being friends, I have a favor to ask you."

Lisa grinned. "Uh-oh. Let's see. You want me to help
with the spring charity auction."

"Hmm, that would be great if you could, but that
wasn't what I had in mind right now. I'm in a pickle. My
guest for Saturday canceled."

Alan was aware that Carrie hosted a live Saturday

morning talk show in the area. *About Portland* usually consisted of human interest stories or timely events.

"How can I help with that?" Lisa asked.

"I'd like you to come on and be my guest. You're intelligent and well-spoken, and I'd like to talk about the opportunities available for young women in Portland who are fresh out of college, settling into the job market now. You'd be great to interview. What do you think?" Carrie was quick to add, "We'd be concentrating on your present job, what you're doing at Summers Development, where you want your future and career to go."

Was that relief he saw on Lisa's face? What did she expect Carrie to interview her about?

"Sure, I can do that. I can even wear one of my new suits."

"You say it's this Saturday?" Brian asked his wife.

"Yes, why?"

"Because Lisa will be traveling to Texas with me and Alan next week. We might be gone the following Saturday. In fact, I was going to ask if you wanted to come along. Alan has room on the plane."

"And there are plenty of guest rooms at the ranch," Alan said encouragingly.

Carrie thought about it, then shook her head. "I'd have to miss the show. I promised Mom I'd take Timothy up to see her and Dad next week. In fact, if you're going to be gone, I could just stay overnight. They'd love that. I think this time it's better if I stay here."

Alan made eye contact with Brian. "What she's really

saying is that she knows you're going to be tied up working most of the time we're gone, and that won't be any fun."

"A man who understands women's subtext," Carrie said with a laugh.

"I've learned a few things in thirty-eight years," he replied.

Why had he stated his age? So that Lisa knew exactly how old he was? So that she realized they were from different generations? Whether there was chemistry between them or not, their age difference probably couldn't be easily bridged.

Probably. Why was he even questioning it?

Lisa pushed her coffee away and laid her napkin on the table. "I'd better collect those things from the attic and load my car. It's getting late and I have laundry to do tonight."

Carrie frowned. "I don't think everything's going to fit in your car. What do you think, Brian?"

"I'll stuff the rest of it in ours and follow her."

"Where do you live?" Alan asked.

"On Chestnut."

"My condo's out that way. And I have an SUV with a back seat that folds down. Whatever doesn't fit in your vehicle can go in mine. I don't mind following you, and it will save Brian a trip."

Alan wasn't exactly sure why he'd offered. Maybe because he wanted to see her place...see if she was paying for it herself, or if it was much too nice for an office manager's salary. Something told him she wasn't

exactly what she seemed. On the other hand, his sixth
sense could just be on alert because she unsettled him.

"I don't have to take everything tonight," she said, a
bit anxiously.

"I really don't mind following you." Alan checked his
watch. "Besides, I should be going, too. There are some
maps and statistics I'd like to go over this evening."

"On the San Diego resort?" Brian asked with a smile.

"That's the one." Standing now, he said to Lisa, "Just
point me to the attic."

Forty-five minutes later, Lisa glanced in her rearview
mirror, wishing she could get her life back under
control. For the past three years she'd let Brian and
Carrie help her, mainly by letting them put her through
college, although she'd worked all she could for
spending money, books, insurance and anything else
she needed. They'd wanted to pay it all, but she'd
already owed them way too much—they'd given her
baby a home.

At school, she'd felt as if she were putting in time, pre-
paring, but not really living the life she wanted to lead.
With graduation, she'd felt on the verge of her future.
Today, when she'd read the anonymous note, *"You owe
me, don't think I've forgotten..."*

Whom did she owe what to?

She'd intended to go home, rearrange some furniture
and think, but now, with Alan Barrett following her...

This was her life and she made the decisions in it. If

she didn't want Alan to stay, she could ask him to leave. Simple, right?

No, not so simple. She had to work with him.

She practically groaned. Yesterday, her life had been easy, moving along its intended course. Today, she didn't know what the next minute was going to bring.

Lisa drove down the tree-lined street of the old neighborhood, pulling up in front of a Victorian that had been divided into two apartments, one downstairs and one upstairs. She had the upper apartment. The rent was modest. Her kitchen linoleum had a crack, and she really should paint her bedroom. There was a stain on the ceiling from when the roof had leaked before she moved in. The grandmotherly lady who owned the property insisted the roof had definitely been fixed. The house brought in income for her, and her grandkids helped with the repairs. The past couple of weekends, Lisa had found a few furnishings and wall decorations at a public sale and at an antique fair. But she still had a way to go and she wasn't keen on Alan seeing the apartment the way it was now.

What *did* it matter?

She hadn't wanted to impress a man since she'd met Thad Preston during her senior year in high school. He'd been the football team's quarterback, headed for the NFL. She'd learned the hard way that he'd intended to let nothing get in the way of that dream.

When she'd told him she was pregnant, he'd insisted she have an abortion. She could never have done that.

And knowing that Aunt Edna would probably kick her out when she learned of the pregnancy, Lisa had saved her the trouble. She'd never wanted to live in Seattle, anyway...*never* liked Seattle. Portland was where she'd grown up, with parents who'd loved her. So that's where she'd returned. She'd gotten a job waitressing, but her morning sickness had soon turned into all-day sickness, forcing her to cut back her hours. Working less, she couldn't afford the room she'd rented. She was out on the streets. Craig, who had managed a local deli, often slipped food to her and her friend Ariel, who'd camped out in vacant buildings with her. He'd also supplied food while they were sleeping at the homeless shelter. But then one day, Lisa had passed out on the street, Ariel had called 911 and she'd been taken to the hospital. The Children's Connection had gotten involved, and that had led to Carrie and Brian.

So who was sending her a threatening note?

Trying to clear her head so she could deal with Alan Barrett, she exited her car and motioned toward the back of the house. "Sorry, but I live upstairs. There's a summer kitchen in the back. You could just unload everything in there."

"And what? You'll carry it up in the morning?"

"It's just end tables and a coffee table, odds and ends."

"You don't like to let anyone do anything for you." He sounded curious more than annoyed.

"If I can do something on my own, why should I ask for help?"

"You're not the damsel in distress type?"

"Not if I can help it."

At that, he laughed and, unfortunately, she liked the sound of it. His laughter was deep and rich, just like his voice. She might as well get this over with, and then he could be on his way, she decided.

They almost had a tug-of-war over the coffee table, the heaviest piece. But Alan was bigger and stronger. When he'd wrestled it from her, he smiled. "Give in, Lisa. Let me take the heavier pieces."

Hands on her hips, she glared up at him. "Are you going to be difficult to work with on the golf resort project, too, Mr. Barrett?"

Holding the coffee table as if it weighed no more than his Stetson, he smiled at her. "It's Alan. And as far as being difficult to work with, that depends on whether you let me have my way or not."

"And I suppose you're used to getting your own way?" she challenged.

"Not many people cross me."

"Then maybe you've met your match."

He eyed her thoroughly. "Maybe. Or maybe because we're both determined and because we both know how to get the job done, we could work very well together."

With a sigh and a shake of her head, she gave in. "Take the coffee table upstairs. I'll grab one of the end tables."

"Why don't you just grab the magazine rack or the flower stand?"

"One thing you're going to learn about me, Mr.—" At

the lift of his brow, she stopped. "Alan…is that I pull my own weight."

"Then go ahead and pull your own weight up there, and unlock the door. You can do that better if you're not carrying anything too heavy."

If she smiled, he'd know he'd won. She wouldn't give him that satisfaction. Instead of the magazine rack or the flower stand, she picked up a floor lamp and hoisted it over her shoulder, then quickly moved ahead of him and hurried toward her apartment. She had to get rid of him. She had to stop reacting to his grin. She had to forget that his eyes were as blue as any sky she'd ever seen.

After several more trips, Lisa quickly positioned everything where she wanted it.

Alan glanced around appreciatively after it was all in place. "You have an eye for arranging furniture."

"I just know where I want it."

His gaze fell on the striped salmon-and-turquoise sofa, the Boston rocker, the mahogany tables and the Tiffany lamp. "You're missing something."

"I know. I need to get an area rug."

"Oh, that's not what I meant. You're missing a big old recliner where someone could be really comfortable."

She assessed him thoughtfully. "Do you have one of those?"

"Back in Texas I do. Here, none of the furniture's quite broken in yet. The recliner has to be five years old to be comfortable."

She couldn't help but move closer to him. She couldn't

help but study his expression carefully. "A man like you keeps a five-year-old recliner?"

"I hold on to things I'm fond of. Just because I can buy anything I want, doesn't mean I'd rather have new than aged. Sort of like that necklace you keep fingering. It doesn't look brand-new, but it seems to mean a lot to you."

She knew whenever she was nervous or uncertain, her locket was a talisman she touched to stay grounded. But she didn't want Alan asking too many questions about it. She certainly wouldn't open it for him.

"This was a gift from Carrie and it means a lot to me. It's an antique. I guess I keep touching it to make sure its still there."

"You're a contradiction."

"And that means...?"

"That means you like to act tough, but I think you've got a softer side."

"You don't know me." She was sure if he did, he would want nothing to do with her.

"We'll be remedying that soon. Working out of town and traveling together has a way of taking off the veneer pretty fast."

The apartment had a quaint older-house smell, part plaster, part polished furniture, part lavender potpourri. But she was standing close enough to Alan to catch the scent of his cologne, to see the interest in his eyes, to feel a pull toward him that made her feel trembly inside.

"Do you live alone at your ranch in Texas?" She wondered what to expect when they got there.

"No, my brother lives there, and I have a housekeeper."

"Does the ranch have a name?" If she didn't keep talking, if she didn't keep words between them, she was afraid something would happen that she'd regret.

"The Lazy B. My grandfather named it and started it on the road to success."

"Why did you get involved in real estate? I mean, wasn't the ranch enough?"

"In some ways, the ranch was *too* much," he drawled. "I grew up there and learned the ropes as a kid. But I also learned it could engulf a man's whole life. I wanted more than that. And since my brother was more inclined to want to handle it, I let him. Christina has always been interested in the horse breeding aspect. It wouldn't surprise me if she wants to take that over someday."

His daughter was merely four years younger than Lisa was. She shouldn't be standing here like this with him, alone in her apartment. She didn't know him. She shouldn't even *want* to know him.

When she took a step back, he asked, "What's wrong?"

"Nothing's wrong. I know you said you have work to do tonight, and I don't want to keep you."

"You suddenly got very nervous on me, Lisa. What's going through your head?"

Since they *did* have to work together, she wasn't about to tell him. "Nothing you want to know about."

"You mean like earlier today? When you got something in the mail and wouldn't tell me why you were upset?"

"As I said, Alan, you don't know me. Maybe you were wrong about my reaction. Maybe you were seeing something that wasn't there."

"Or maybe you're trying to hide how disturbed you were by that piece of mail."

She took a couple more steps back, knowing that this man saw entirely too much. "I think you'd better go."

Cocking his head, he asked gently, "Are you afraid of me, Lisa?"

"Should I be?" Her question was almost belligerent. She needed to wrap defenses around herself, and that was the only one she could find.

"Hell, no. I like women. I respect them. And I think I can read the signals they give out pretty well."

"I'm not giving out any signals."

"You're doing a terrific job of trying not to." He shrugged. "As you said, we're going to be working together. If we establish a friendship, that will be a lot easier."

A friendship? Like she had with Craig? She doubted that. Everything about Alan shouted, *I'm a powerful male and used to getting my own way.* She had a habit of defying any man who tried to patronize her or wear a mantle of authority around her.

"Just think about it," Alan suggested, as if whatever decision she came to didn't matter to him at all. "I promise you, you're safe around me, Lisa. After all, I have a daughter who's only a few years younger than you."

In plain English, he was telling her he was as aware of their age difference as she was. If there was an attraction between them, it wouldn't go anywhere. There were simply too many complications.

He moved toward the door. As he opened it, he said, "Good luck with your interview on Saturday. Carrie invited me to stop and watch her work. I might just do that. Good night, Lisa."

Then Alan Barrett was gone.

Touching her locket, rubbing her thumb over the engraved front of it, Lisa sank down onto the couch. She wasn't keen to do this interview in the first place. Now, knowing he might be there…

She felt as if she had so many secrets to hide, she couldn't keep the door shut on all of them. Somehow she had to. Alan's opinion of her was already important to her, and that worried her most of all.

Chapter Three

"Do you know if it's cool in Rocky Ridge, Texas this time of year?" Jillian Logan asked Lisa as they shopped in one of Portland's department stores Friday evening.

Lisa plucked a burgundy plaid blouse from a rack and held it in front of her. "I looked it up on the Internet. It's possible they can even get snow in February, so wearing long sleeves won't be a problem."

"Tell me again why you don't want this Alan Barrett to see your tattoos?"

Jillian, who was twelve years older than Lisa, had become like a big sister since they'd gotten to know one another. Jillian was a social worker at the Children's Connection, and Lisa had met her after she had given up Timothy for adoption. They'd clicked, and Jillian was one of the few people who knew Lisa's whole story.

"I'll be working with him," Lisa replied. "He has to see me as a professional."

"I think it's more than that. You don't want him to ask any questions."

Sensitive and caring, Jillian was insightful, too…at least about everyone else. Jillian and her twin brother David had been abandoned by their drug-addicted mother and left in the care of their grandmother, a stroke victim who was barely able to care for them. Thanks to the support and love of the Logans, Jillian and David had survived and thrived. But Jillian was shy in her personal life. She could fight for a client, no holds barred, but when it came to herself and men, she lacked confidence.

"I *don't* want any questions," Lisa admitted. "It seems Alan has been working with Brian a lot."

"Alan, is it?" Jillian asked with a sly smile.

Not much flustered Lisa, but Alan Barrett did—even a simple discussion about him.

"I don't believe it." Jillian's smile was wide. "You're blushing!"

Embarrassed, Lisa returned the blouse to the rack. "No, I'm not. It's just hot in here."

Jillian's brown eyes were kind as she tapped her friend's shoulder. "What's going on?"

With a huge sigh, Lisa answered honestly, "He ties me in knots. Do you know what I mean?"

"Uh-oh. How much time have you spent with him?"

"Not very much. I sat in on a meeting with him in Brian's office and had dinner with him at Brian and Carrie's. When we go on this trip to Texas, I'll be with him every day for three or four days. What am I going to do? I don't want him to see how he affects me. I have to be all business."

"Do you?"

"What do you mean?"

Her friend eyed her assessingly. "There's a reason he's tying you in knots. A *non*business reason. Why does he unsettle you?"

"If I knew, I could stop it from happening," Lisa grumbled.

Jillian gave her a penetrating look.

"Okay, let me think about it. He's got the bluest eyes I've ever seen. He's tall and broad shouldered and makes me feel protected, which is crazy, because I've only been around him about two minutes. He's got this deep voice that just kind of seeps under my skin, and a Texas accent that for some reason makes my heart beat faster. On the other hand, he's much older than I am. Before you start analyzing and telling me I'm looking for a father figure, forget it, because when I look at him—"

"How much older?" Jillian asked, cutting right to the chase.

"Seventeen years older."

Her friend whistled through her teeth. "Lisa…"

"We started out on the wrong foot," Lisa admitted. "He

had this authority thing going on and was determined he could do whatever he wanted. But I stopped him cold."

"Yeah, I would imagine that. You and authority figures don't mesh well."

"But then he helped me carry some furniture up to my apartment and that authority thing wasn't part of it at all. I mean, when I'm around him, I don't even think about him being older."

"You'd better watch your step."

"Nothing's going to happen, Jillian. You know me." She lowered her voice. "I haven't even *been* with anyone since Thad. I mean, I don't know if I'd even remember what to do."

Jillian rolled her eyes. "I think it would all come back."

Lisa shook her head vehemently. "I don't want it to come back. I don't want to get involved with anyone."

"I'm not sure that's true," her friend said. "You want to get involved but you're afraid if you do, the man will walk away and you'll have to deal with abandonment again. You've been abandoned a lot."

Yes, she had—by her parents when they died, by her aunt when she didn't want her, by Thad, who hadn't really cared about her at all. Thinking of him made Lisa remember the note. Thinking about the note made anxiety turn in her stomach. She could confide in Jillian, she supposed, but something made her keep the letter to herself. As long as she didn't tell anyone about it, it didn't seem real.

Taking a deep breath, willfully lightening her mood,

she asked Jillian, "Are you giving me a free counseling session?"

"If you need one."

"I don't. Alan is Brian's colleague and just somebody I have to work with on this project. We'll both be professional and when we're at his ranch in Texas, Brian will be a great chaperone. I have nothing to worry about."

"Repeat it a thousand more times, and I might believe it."

If she repeated it a thousand more times, she might believe it herself, Lisa thought. She pointed to a light blue and white striped shirt with embroidery on the pockets. Going to the display rack, she found her size and held it up. "What do you think?"

"I think you're trying to concentrate on details so you don't have to think about the trip itself."

Sometimes Lisa wished Jillian wasn't quite so perceptive. But if she needed to think about the details to alleviate some of her anxiety, that was exactly what she was going to do.

"My career is everything to me now," Lisa told Carrie during their TV interview on Saturday morning.

Carrie had spent the last twenty minutes going over Lisa's degree, future goals and the opportunities in Portland for young professionals. In her charming way, she had kept the interview questions nonpersonal but interesting, so Lisa could give information to young people making decisions about college.

Now, however, her voice warmed into a teasing quality. "Everything?" she asked with a smile. "A beautiful young woman like yourself makes time for dating, I imagine. Are there opportunities for young professionals to meet in Portland?"

Lisa felt heat come into her cheeks. "There are clubs and organizations." She realized Carrie had to give the viewers something a little more personal than her career to pique their interest. But she had to admit dating wasn't on her agenda, even though Carrie thought it should be. "I really don't date. There just doesn't seem to be time in my schedule. Some evenings I get home late, weekends I catch up on chores and spend time with family and friends."

"I imagine the station might get a few e-mails from young men who are interested in you. What would you say to them?"

"I'd say my focus is on building my future and the future of the family I'd like to have someday. I don't have time for romantic entanglements right now. I'm operating on the belief that I'm self-sufficient. I have my own apartment, pay my own bills, pay my own way. The truth is, I don't really want a man complicating my life."

"In other words, you want to be financially stable before you enter into a partnership with anyone."

"Exactly," Lisa agreed. "I don't want any of my decisions to be impulsive ones, but well thought out. That way, they won't land me in trouble." *Again,* she thought, determined not to make the same mistake she'd made before. When she was a high school senior she'd needed someone to love, and she'd needed someone to love her. Only Thad hadn't loved her, he'd used her.

She wouldn't fall into that trap again.

"It's been a pleasure interviewing you, Lisa," Carrie said, meaning it. "You've given young women goals to aspire to. Thank you for agreeing to be on *About Portland*."

Then the camera focused on Carrie, and Lisa could finally relax. Carrie had danced on the edge of the personal, but taken care not to ask questions that would reveal anything Lisa preferred to keep to herself.

After Carrie signed off, she stood and removed her microphone. Lisa did the same and set it on the chair where she'd sat. The bright lights that had blinded her suddenly blinked off.

A male voice came from the side of the room—a deep male voice Lisa was beginning to know all too well.

"Great job, Miss Sanders." Although he'd called her by her first name a few times, he obviously felt the need for more formality today. As he approached the stage, his rugged good looks practically bowled her over, and she felt that pull of attraction again.

"Alan! I'm glad you dropped by," Carrie said. "What did you think of the interview?"

His gaze stayed on Lisa as he answered, "I picked up some pointers for Christina. After all, if I'm going to spend more time in Portland, she might want to consider getting a job in this area after college."

"So you're really going to establish roots here?" Carrie asked.

Finally he broke eye contact. "It seems that way. I suppose it depends on the market, but the development deals Brian and I are making will last for many years. Have you two ladies had breakfast? I'd be glad to treat."

"That would be wonderful," Carrie responded with a smile. "Lisa and I are going to run errands, but we can take a little time for breakfast, right?"

As Carrie checked with her, Lisa knew she couldn't nix the idea. This man was Brian's colleague. And Carrie was only doing her part to help Brian. "Right," she answered brightly.

No sense trying to wiggle out of breakfast. She could keep herself removed. She could pretend that Alan was just a business client who had to be entertained for half an hour.

"I have to go to the dressing room and pick up a few things I left there," Carrie stated. "Anything I can gather up for you?"

Lisa's purse was lying to the side of the stage under a coat she'd tossed over a chair. "No, I'm fine."

"I'll be right back." Carrie flashed another one of those smiles that could bring any man to his knees. The thing was, she didn't seem to care how beautiful she was, or that lots of men looked at her with longing. She only cared about how Brian looked at her. Lisa loved that about her.

To Lisa's surprise, Alan's gaze was back on her rather than on Carrie walking away. "So real estate really is where you want to build your future?"

Had he thought she'd been kidding, merely using this job with Brian as a stepping stone? In a way she was. "I want to get experience with Brian, but I have another goal, too, and because of that I'll probably leave Summers Development eventually. I'd like to hook up with a contractor to develop communities for families. There are several in California that are great models."

"You mean planned communities?"

"Yes. A real neighborhood, where people know each other, where there's a park with a playground for kids to play, where the school is close enough to walk to. I don't want to create an exclusive neighborhood with gates and security men, but a place where everyone watches out for everyone else."

"That has a lot more to do with people than the land they're building houses on," he said with understanding.

"Maybe. But I think with the right public relations, with the right focus, we'll draw in buyers who want that kind of neighborhood. I don't care if I get rich doing it. I just want to make a difference." As soon as those words were out of her mouth, she knew Alan could take them as an insult. "Not that there's anything wrong with being rich," she amended quickly.

Instead of being insulted, he laughed, and she could feel the pleasure of the sound down to the tips of her high-heeled shoes.

"Do you always say exactly what you're feeling?" he asked with curiosity, a smile still on his lips…very nice male lips. Today he was dressed in gray, stone-washed jeans and a navy-blue sweater. A hint of blond chest hair peeked out of his V-neck.

Lisa felt that hot tingly feeling rolling through her again. "Usually. I think it's important for people to know where I stand. So there's no misunderstanding. Misunderstandings are inevitable, but honesty helps."

"And you really don't date? That man who took you to lunch looked very friendly."

"That's because we *are* friends."

Now Alan's voice turned from amused to serious. "What turned you off men?"

"I'm not turned off men. I'm just focused on my career."

He gave her a long look.

"Really, Mr. Barrett. I'm just very focused."

"It's Alan, remember? And do you mind if I call you Lisa?"

"No, I don't mind," she said softly.

As they gazed at each other for a few moments, Lisa felt the rest of the world falling away. Her knees seemed a little wobbly and she wondered if someone had sucked all the oxygen out of the room.

"This community you want to build. Would you like to do that in California?"

His question brought her back to reality. "Oh, no." She thought about Timothy and Carrie and Brian. "I don't intend to leave Portland. I have close friends here."

"I would have thought a career woman on the move would relocate in order to further her ambition."

"I was born and raised in Portland, and Portland is where I want to stay. Maybe fifteen years from now I'll consider branching out."

"Why fifteen?"

Lisa knew she'd just made a huge mistake. In her mind, she thought about when Timothy would be eighteen and going off to college. And if college wasn't what he wanted, he might travel or move someplace else. Fifteen years from now, she still wanted to be his friend. Long before then, she hoped, he'd know she was his mother. She'd go wherever was necessary to maintain contact.

"Fifteen years seems reasonable to accomplish what I want to do here," she ad-libbed.

But Alan seemed to be a perceptive man, and the look he gave her said he knew she was hiding something, or if not hiding it, guarding her privacy all too well. Well, he'd just have to wonder. She didn't discuss her past with anyone unless they'd lived it with her. She didn't want to revisit it, although it was always right behind her. When she thought about the threatening note she'd received, she wanted to blank it all out, and that's exactly what she was going to do, for as long as she could.

Alan Barrett didn't need to know anything more about her in order to work with her. And that's *all* they were going to do—work together.

Alan pushed open the heavy door to the Goal Post, an out-of-the-way pub in Portland. The early February rain had pelted his windshield on his drive over. He was glad to escape from the dampness into the bar, which boasted a real fireplace. Brian had introduced him to the Goal Post after one of their first successful deals. Now Alan had named it as a meeting place for him and an old college buddy, Gil Reynolds. He and Gil had gotten together last fall after Alan had started spending a lot of time in Portland, but since then, they'd both been too busy to connect.

Alan spotted Gil at a bleacher-style booth, not far from the fireplace. As he approached, Gil grinned. His dark brown hair looked damp, and his black eyes looked as sharp and calculating as they had when they'd been housemates off campus at the University of Oregon.

Alan slid onto the hard wooden seat across from Gil. "It's good to see you, finally. How have you been?"

"Busy, the same as you. You know the newspaper business."

Gil was an editor at the *Portland Gazette*. "Real estate and news," Alan commented. "I guess we're both in careers that never let up."

"That's the truth. Not only do they never let up, but to sell papers I have to keep coming up with bigger stories. Do you know what I mean?"

"Yeah, I think I do. Clients aren't any easier to please these days than advertisers or subscribers. And as we both know, bigger isn't always better."

When the waitress came to their table, they both ordered beer on tap.

"So how's Christina?" Gil asked. "Is she enjoying her last year of high school? Are you ready for her to fly off on her own?"

"She's loving her last year, and, no, I'm not ready for her to leave. To tell you the truth, I can't quite imagine her not being at the ranch on weekends. I can't imagine her only coming home on holidays. I can't imagine worrying because she's not with her mother and she's not with me and God knows what she is doing."

"I thought you said Christina has a level head."

"She does, usually, but put her at college with all that freedom, with new friends, with guys who want to take advantage of her, and I think I'd rather lock her in her room for a couple of more years."

Gil laughed. "You are the definition of a protective father. How does she put up with you?"

"I try to hide my protective streak when she's around."

"I don't think you fool her for a minute. And how's Sherri?"

"Sherri is Sherri," Alan said with a shrug. "She flits from one new project to another. She's on a committee to beautify the roads and historic buildings in Rocky Ridge. Her new hobby is making jewelry out of glass beads, and she's thinking about staying on as the cheerleading coach even after Christina graduates. From what Christina tells me, she has a new boyfriend. This one is a stockbroker."

"Is it serious?"

"You expect me to know that?"

"You and Sherri talk."

"About Christina, not about our personal lives."

"Do you have a personal life?" Gil asked, with the interest of a longtime friend.

In spite of himself, Alan thought of Lisa. "I don't have time for one."

"As the most eligible bachelor in Rocky Ridge, you might have dated every single woman there. But now that you've come to Portland, you have a whole new dating pool. Every man needs a little recreation."

For a certain number of years after his divorce, Alan and Gil had had the same mind-set about dating. Women could relieve the pressure of a heavy workload, while providing entertainment, companionship and physical satisfaction. But over the past few years, Alan had found that seeing women in that light, not attempting to find anything deeper, had left him empty, restless and feeling more alone than he had after his divorce. So instead of putting his energy into being charming and attentive to a woman for an evening, he'd discovered he'd found more enjoyment in traveling someplace he'd never been, going white-water rafting or simply riding his favorite horse until the wind blew the cobwebs from his head.

"I'm not interested in Portland's dating pool." Nevertheless, he thought again of Lisa—how poised she was, how frank, how the camera had seemed to love her face during her interview. Once more, he pushed her from his mind.

"Are *you* seeing anybody regularly?" he asked Gil.

"That all depends on what you mean by regularly."

"You know, the same woman one weekend after another for more than a month."

Instead of the sardonic smile Gil was so good at, he frowned and moved the saltshaker back and forth on the table. "I don't know, Alan. I start liking a woman. We have fun together. We have a good time in bed. Then something happens. Suddenly we're not just dating. We're a couple and then I hear things like, 'Maybe you could stay overnight more often, maybe I could stay with you more often, why don't you give me a key, why don't we move in together, you should meet my parents, I should meet yours, have you thought about having a family?'"

"In other words, the woman wants more."

"Yeah, that's right. The woman wants more. I don't. Some days I go into work at six and I don't get home until ten, twelve, two. I've got a career and it's damn demanding. My personal life has always come second, but a woman never wants to hear that."

"Tell me something, Gil. Is your career just a ready excuse not to get involved with anybody?"

"You tell me. Don't you do the same thing?"

"Not anymore. As I said, I'm not even looking at the dating pool. I've found other ways to enjoy life. But you like parties. You like going clubbing."

The waitress brought them mugs of beer and Gil raised his to Alan. "You're right. I do. I like having fun."

"That's why you shut down and make an exit when a woman wants more?"

Gil's eyes narrowed and he lifted his mug. "Uh-oh. We're getting way too deep here. Maybe you're asking me all these questions because you're looking for answers yourself."

Was he looking for answers to the void in his life that would yawn wide open when Christina went to college? Why hadn't *he* gotten involved with anyone seriously since his divorce? Why had meeting Lisa Sanders shaken him up in a way he didn't understand at all?

"One more question, then we can move on to how the Mariners are going to do this year," Alan promised.

Gil took a few swallows of beer, then set down his mug. "Shoot. But I reserve the right to remain silent."

"Have you ever dated a younger woman?"

Gil smiled. "How much younger?"

"I don't know, maybe ten, twelve, fifteen years younger."

"I've dated a few women in their mid-twenties, but we seemed to run out of things to say. Our reference points were different. Do you know what I mean?"

Alan understood what Gil was saying, yet when he talked with Lisa, he didn't feel any of that.

"Are you thinking about dating someone younger?" Gil asked.

Now wasn't *that* a million dollar question. Alan lifted his mug, too. "I was just hypothesizing."

"You don't hypothesize. You act. You're a doer, not a ponderer. So if there's a younger woman who's making you ponder, you could be in big trouble already."

Gil was an intelligent man and thought of himself as a cynical reporter feeding the public's right to know. He had a sixth sense about a good story and could be perceptive about everybody but himself. This time Alan hoped Gil's insight into what was going on with *him* was all wrong.

But the devil on Alan's shoulder told him his friend was on the money once again.

Chapter Four

"Brian left about a half hour ago, Alan."

Lisa kept her voice completely professional as they spoke over the phone late Monday afternoon. On Saturday, during breakfast with Alan after her interview, she'd let Carrie lead the conversation. However, her gaze had locked with his too many times and her heart had beat much too fast whenever he'd spoken to her…whenever she'd spoken to him.

"I was hoping I could catch him before he left." Frustration edged Alan's tone. "I have the schematics he wanted for that San Diego resort. I suppose I could have them messengered to his house."

"No! I mean," she added quickly, "I can come over and pick them up."

She *had* to convince Alan not to interrupt Brian tonight. Brian had shown her the flowers he'd picked up at lunchtime to take home to Carrie, a dozen long-stemmed red roses. Since they were leaving Wednesday for the trip to Texas, and tomorrow night would be busy with last minute preparations, Lisa suspected he and Carrie were going to have some quality time tonight after Timothy went to bed. If they were interrupted by a messenger service, their evening could be ruined. She had a key to the house. She could pick up the materials from Alan and drop them off without Brian and Carrie even noticing. She'd leave them in Brian's office with a note and slip out again before they even knew she had been there.

"I hate to take you out of your way. If I can't find a service to do this tonight, I could drive them over to Brian myself," Alan offered.

"Aren't you working on the presentation for the investors?"

"Did Brian tell you that?"

"He gave me a schedule of our meetings with clients, what he was covering and what you're covering. I know you're busy. My evening's free. I really don't mind stopping by. Just give me directions and tell me exactly where you live."

After a brief hesitation, Alan did just that.

A half hour later, the security guard at Alan's building showed Lisa to a private elevator that went directly to the penthouse floor. Alan had apparently given the man her name and told him she'd be arriving within the hour.

The elevator was smooth and speedy, rushing her to the seventh floor in a matter of seconds. When the doors parted, she stepped out into a hallway with plush wine carpeting. The paintings that hung along the corridor were watercolors of ranch scenes.

When she stopped before one and studied it, she saw Christina Barrett's signature in the corner. Obviously Alan was proud of everything his daughter did.

Lisa had almost reached the paneled mahogany door of the penthouse when it opened and he stood there, looking like neither a businessman nor a Texas rancher. Dressed in khakis and a long-sleeved, black Henley shirt, his rough-hewn face shadowed by a beard line, he looked too sexy for words and not altogether glad to see her. His blue eyes assessed her. She knew he couldn't see much, because she'd buttoned and belted her coat against the inclement weather.

"Didn't you park in the garage?"

"I found a spot across the street and just dashed over. I'm not fond of parking garages. They make me feel claustrophobic."

"That surprises me. You give the impression you're not afraid of anything."

"I didn't say I was *afraid* of parking garages. I just prefer not to park in them."

He held up a staying hand. "I shouldn't have made the observation. I don't really know you. I've just gotten a few impressions."

She'd gotten a few impressions of her own. Alan, for all his charming Texas manners, was a bit of a loner. How she knew that she wasn't sure. Maybe he was different around family. Maybe his daughter knew the real man underneath. But Lisa didn't suppose many people did.

He motioned her inside. "If you want to warm up a bit before you dash back out there, I have a fresh pot of coffee brewing."

Having coffee with Alan—in his apartment, no less— wasn't a good idea. Coming here had been a *bad* idea. Still, she looked around with interest. "No, I'll just pick up whatever you want Brian to look at, then I'll be going."

Alan's condo was a showplace. The same rich carpeting from the hall covered the living room. A navy leather couch and huge recliner were arranged across from a high-tech entertainment center, plasma screen TV, stereo system, CD player. Other electronic gadgets sat on the shelves—an iPod and an Xbox, along with a rack of CDs. The buttered plaster walls were devoid of art. She could see into the dining room with its shiny mahogany table that looked as if it had never been used. Alan might stay here when he was in Portland, but he didn't really live here. It was too uncluttered, too clean, too polished.

He went to the library table along one wall and picked up a cardboard tube. Handing it to her, he asked, "What's the real reason you wanted to pick these up?"

His perception amazed her. She'd found most men accepted simple explanations and didn't look much deeper. But she was discovering that Alan wasn't like most men.

To be diplomatic or just plain honest?

With this man, she went with honesty. "Brian was planning to spend some time with Carrie tonight."

Alan's eyebrows quirked up. "What are you, their guardian angel?"

That was laughable. She wasn't anybody's angel. Not by a long shot. "I'm a friend," she answered easily. "That's all."

The truth was, she remembered the tension between Brian and Carrie before they'd adopted Timothy. A lot of that tension had come from Carrie inviting Lisa into their home to live until her child was born. But since then, Carrie had confided in Lisa that the tension had come from the secret Carrie had kept from Brian throughout their marriage, until the night Timothy had been kidnapped. The trauma of that awful event had brought everything out in the open. Afterward, when Brian had come to terms with all of it, his marriage to Carrie had become stronger than it had ever been. So had his commitment and his love. When Timothy had been returned to them, well cared for and healthy, they'd been ready for a new stage in their lives and in their marriage. Lisa admired them as individuals and as a couple.

Apparently deciding to take a different tack, Alan handed her the cardboard tube. "Are you ready to go to Texas?"

"Do you mean am I ready to fly in a private jet, or am I ready to absorb everything about this development deal so that I'll learn from it and move on to the next step?"

"Both."

"I'm ready." She tilted her head and added, "I even bought a pair of cowboy boots."

At that he laughed, and the tension that always seemed to crop up between them eased. "Have you ever been on a working ranch?" he asked.

"Nope. I've been a city girl all my life. Do you think I'll have some time to see what you do there?"

"Oh, I think you'll have time to fit in a tour. If I'm too busy, Neal can show you around."

"If you're busy with this golf resort, *I* will be, too."

"That isn't exactly what I meant. Besides work, I'll be spending some time with my daughter. I always do when I'm home."

Lisa knew she shouldn't set foot in dangerous territory. She knew she should leave well enough alone. Yet she couldn't help herself. "You must have been young when you became a father."

He was standing very close to her now. Chest hairs peeked up over the buttons of his shirt. It was so tempting… She curled her hand around the schematics tube. This man oozed so much sex appeal he almost took her breath away.

"I was young. Twenty-one," he explained. "But from the moment I learned I was going to be a father, it was as if my life crystalized around the baby—around Christina. I left college and didn't look back."

"You left?" That surprised her. Alan was quick, intelligent, perceptive. To her, that had added up to well-educated.

"I could have worked on the ranch and just pulled a salary, but I wanted more for the family I was building.

I helped manage the Lazy B and finished learning the ropes, but at night I got my real estate license. By the time Christina was in grade school, I already had a nest egg squirreled away."

Obviously he hadn't thought of giving the responsibility for his daughter to someone else. It sounded as if he'd taken on his new life without a complaint, without fear, without regret. There was no doubt in Lisa's mind now that he'd never understand why she'd given up a baby for adoption. There was no doubt that if he knew, he'd no longer respect her.

"What's the matter?" he asked, stepping even closer. "You look as if you've lost your best friend."

Steeling herself, she met his gaze. To steer the conversation away from children, she replied with a question to turn the focus back on him. "So you never finished your degree?"

"Never did. Maybe when I retire, or when I'm too old to climb on a horse, I'll have the time. I decided real life experience was worth twenty years of book learning any day. You'll see that for yourself now that you're in the thick of it."

She certainly was in the thick of it. His blue eyes were absolutely mesmerizing. The timbre of his deep voice strummed a chord somewhere in her midsection. She responded to him viscerally and she hated the fact she couldn't control her reaction.

When he reached out and lightly trailed his fingers along a loose strand of her hair, she didn't breathe.

"It's wet." His voice was husky and low.

"It'll dry," she managed to say, still caught up in him. She'd forgotten why she'd come to his condo.

He dropped his hand to his side. "You're so young."

"Isn't age a state of mind?" she asked, more seriously than flippantly.

"I wish that were true."

"You're not old," she protested.

"No, I'm not. But I'm not fresh out of college, either. My life's on a track I've already chosen. Yours still has a lot of flexibility."

Was he going to talk about this attraction? Were they going to admit there was some kind of live current between them?

For an instant—just an instant—she thought he might bend his head and kiss her. She thought they might find out exactly what the chemistry was between them. But maybe that was the difference between her being twenty-one and him being thirty-eight. He didn't want to risk finding out.

Stepping back, he slipped his hands into his slacks pockets. "Tell Brian I'll talk to him during the flight to Texas about the changes I think we should make."

"You won't see him before then?"

"No, I have meetings all day tomorrow. Tomorrow night I want to check out the plane myself and make sure everything's ready."

A hum of intense awareness still danced between them. He'd stepped away from it and she knew she should, too. This time she did.

As she walked toward the door, he followed her.

"When you enter the elevator, Ralph will be alerted downstairs. He'll escort you out of the building."

Now Alan couldn't seem to wait to get her out of his apartment. Maybe he'd been closer to kissing her than she'd imagined. Or maybe he was just a busy man with a workload she'd never want to contemplate.

At his door she turned the knob and opened it. "I'll see you Wednesday morning."

He nodded, his expression set and serious. "See you Wednesday morning," he agreed and closed his door behind her.

As Lisa walked toward the elevator, she still felt the intimacy of standing near Alan. The thrill of awareness of looking at him, breathing in his cologne, still surged through her system. But again she caught sight of Christina's name on a watercolor in the hall. Alan Barrett had embraced fatherhood as he had everything else in his life, and he was proud of it.

Lisa knew he'd never be proud of *her.*

When Lisa stepped inside Alan's plane, she felt almost awed. It wasn't just the smell of fine leather, the computer workstations, the space. It was the atmosphere. Big deals happened for Alan even here.

"Have you been inside a corporate jet before?" His deep voice came from an alcove, which, she saw, was a galley of sorts. He was dressed in a plaid shirt, jeans and the ever-present boots.

"I've never been inside anything like this, but I guess if you do business all over the country, it's the best way to travel."

"I found it to be. Let me give you a tour. I want you to feel at home. If you need something during the flight, please help yourself." He motioned to the refrigerator in the alcove. "It's well stocked with soda, wine, beer and fruit juice."

Opening the cupboards above it, he pointed out crackers and cookies and peanut butter. "For longer trips we pack frozen dinners, but this will only take us three and a half hours." He noticed her briefcase and purse. "Did you hand off your suitcase down below?"

"Yes, someone took it before I came up the stairs. I guess Brian's not here yet? He told me to take a taxi, and I think Carrie's going to drop him off."

Moving toward one of the high-back, camel leather seats, Alan pointed to the workstation in front of it. "You can stow your things there if you like."

She did and then pulled down the short jacket of her denim pantsuit. The long sleeves covered both of her tattoos and that's the way she wanted it.

After Alan showed her where the bathroom was located, he glanced at the curtain at the back of the plane. So did she. When he swung aside the fabric, which slid across a rod, Lisa spotted a bed.

"Sometimes I have to catch a few winks," he explained. "It comes in handy."

The bed brought to mind images she didn't want to

think about. Images of Alan shirtless. More than shirtless. Then she wondered if he brought along women on
any of those jaunts. This alcove could be a secluded
hideaway, flying high above the rest of the world,
immune from it, separate from it....

"What are you thinking?"

Flustered, she quickly mumbled, "Nothing. I mean...
it's convenient for you to have this here."

When he moved close to her, she took a step back. He
frowned. "You're jumpy today. What's going on?"

After taking a steadying breath, she met his gaze. "In
lots of ways, this is like a job interview for me. I'm an
apprentice, learning the ropes. At least that's the way I
look at it. I don't want to do anything wrong or say
anything wrong."

Angling his head, he eyed her thoughtfully. "You seem
to have a level head on your shoulders. You know what
you want. You're well-spoken and seem to quickly grasp
whatever Brian and I discuss. You're not going to say or
do anything wrong."

"I don't mean so much professionally as...personally."

"Let's be honest, Lisa. I think there's chemistry going
on between us that neither of us wants to admit to. But
I'll tell you this. If you want no part of it, you just say
so. I understand 'no.' I understand 'business only.'"

If she admitted to the attraction between them, she had
a feeling she'd be in *big* trouble.

Just then, Brian boarded the plane. Lisa breathed a hefty
sigh of relief. Alan heard it, but he misunderstood it.

"Maybe I've gotten things all wrong. Maybe what's really afoot here is chemistry between you and Brian."

Shocked, Lisa was speechless for a moment.

Brian stopped at one of the chairs to unload his briefcase. Lisa wanted to protest. She wanted to tell Alan he couldn't be more wrong. But she couldn't discuss it with him while Brian was within earshot.

Alan was already turning away, and she knew he thought he'd gotten it right. As soon as she could, she had to set him straight. But she needed a little privacy to do that. She might also need one huge dose of courage, because she might have to admit that the sparks between her and Alan were quite real.

Lisa stayed very much in the background as the two men discussed business during the flight to Rocky Ridge, Texas. Alan looked at her and even Brian differently, and she hated that. She had to put things straight with him— and soon—but she didn't want Brian to have any inkling of what Alan thought.

When they flew over the town of Rocky Ridge, heading south to the airport, Brian was the one to point out a few landmarks—the mall, the medical clinic, the sheriff's department, the high school from which Christina would soon be graduating.

After they landed, Alan spent a few minutes talking with the pilot. A black SUV pulled up to the plane and Alan introduced his brother, Neal, who was two inches shorter, and stockier. Neal's hair was brown rather than blond, but his eyes were the same vivid blue as Alan's.

He shook Brian's hand enthusiastically. When Lisa extended hers, he gave it a quick shake, apparently dismissing her as an underling. Normally her hackles would rise at something like that, but she was too worried about the conversation she had to have with Alan to be concerned with what his brother thought. After all, she was simply a secretary on this trip, wasn't she?

Neal drove a few miles from the airport, then veered onto a drive that passed under a wooden arch branded with the Lazy B. The road and white pipe fencing seemed to go on for miles. Eventually they arrived at a sprawling, tan brick house two stories tall and grander than any Lisa had ever seen. Carrie and Brian's home was spacious, but this was magnificent.

As Alan showed them inside, they entered a huge living room. She could see the dining room and kitchen beyond.

Alan pointed toward the left. "There's a family room with a pool table over that way." He nodded to the right. "Down that hall, you'll find a home theater, library and exercise room. Neal has the east wing upstairs and I have the west wing. The guest rooms are in the middle above the main part of the house. Maude will show you to your rooms. I have to make a few calls, then we can meet in the dining room for lunch."

"Sounds good," Brian said. "I'll put in a call to Carrie once I unpack."

Alan seemed to give his friend an extra long look. "Miss her already?"

Brian grinned. "Sure do. This will be a long few days."

Alan took a quick glance at Lisa as the housekeeper came into the living room and he introduced her. Maude Swenson, a short woman with a gray braid wrapped around the top of her head, beamed at them. "It's so nice to have company. Let me get you settled in." To Lisa she said, "Since this is your first time here, I gave you the best room in the house. You have a balcony that overlooks the pool. Come on, let me show you some of the reasons why we love the Lazy B so much."

Since Brian knew his way around, Maude spent her time with Lisa. The room she showed her to was filled with pansies—pansy wallpaper, a white eyelet spread sprinkled with pansies and thick lavender carpeting that stopped just short of the ceramic tile threshold to the balcony. As Maude opened the French doors, Lisa realized she had never seen a property like this with a pool and pool house, barns and outbuildings, cows lowing in the distance, horses running in the corrals. This was a world she'd never known nor could ever hope to know. But it would be lovely to spend a short time here.

Maude confided that she'd come to the Lazy B after Alan's momma had died when he was ten. Not having any family of her own, she'd found a home here, and had never regretted devoting her life to the Barretts. She told Lisa to take her time coming downstairs and to feel free to look around if she liked. Nothing was off-limits, except, of course, for the brothers' master suites.

Lisa wasn't about to go anywhere near Alan's suite

and she had the feeling she wasn't going to have much contact with Neal.

It didn't matter. Alan's family was no concern of hers.

After she unpacked, she went downstairs and soon found herself in the game room. It was wallpapered in a red-and-navy diamond design. One of the side walls was covered with framed photographs, and she went over to study them. She soon figured out the pictures were of generations of Barretts and what they'd accomplished. There were men in Daniel Boone hats, cowboy hats and black derbies. They had handlebar mustaches, full beards and sour expressions. Interspersed among the portraits were sepia pictures of oil wells, cattle roundups and early days in Rocky Ridge.

"Studying those pictures is like taking a walk back into history."

Lisa turned to see Alan coming in. His strides were quick and sure. He still wasn't smiling, and stopped when he stood beside her. "What do you think of the Lazy B?"

"I think it's more ranch than I would ever know what to do with."

He gave her a wry smile. "It's two handfuls, that's for sure, but Neal does a good job of managing it. We have reliable help we depend on." Turning toward her then, he asked, "Do you like your room?"

"It's beautiful. It tempts me to just settle in and stay awhile."

The silence between them became awkward, and Lisa knew she had to step into it. Postponing the discussion they had to have, she said, "Maude told me she started working here after your mother died. She said you were ten."

"Maude's been a second mother to me."

"Do you mind me asking how your mother died?"

"I don't mind. She was killed in a riding accident. One of those freak things. She was thrown from her horse and hit her head."

"I'm so sorry."

"Fortunately, I was old enough to remember her. I have lots of good memories. Maybe we've kept them alive because of all the photographs we have, but sometimes, especially when I'm in the barn, I think I can still hear her laughter. That was one of her favorite places to be."

Lisa nodded slowly. "I lost both of my parents at the same time in a car accident. I was fifteen, so I have a lot of memories, too. Nothing tangible though, except a pearl ring of my mom's, and decorations my dad received when he was in the service."

"What happened to the rest?"

"My aunt sold it to have the funds to take care of me."

Alan's gaze was kind. "That's when you went to live in Seattle?"

Somehow she'd slipped into giving more personal information than she'd wanted to. She had to remember this man didn't miss a thing—and he seemed to remember *everything*.

"Yes." To prevent further probing, she got straight to the point. "Alan, I think you've jumped to the wrong conclusion about Brian and me. When he and Carrie found out I had no family to speak of, they befriended me. I'm close to *both* of them."

Alan studied her. "Brian gave you a job. You babysit for them. You're close to them, supposedly, but Brian never mentioned you during the time we've been working together. I wonder why that is."

Obviously, Alan thought it was because Brian might have feelings for her he wanted to keep hidden. He didn't. He didn't discuss her because of Timothy's adoption and his desire to respect her privacy.

"Apparently you weren't around when I was home from school," she suggested. "I spent my holidays with Brian and Carrie, but I guess you were here in Texas then."

After thinking about it, Alan nodded. "I guess I was. *And* for the whole month of January. The truth is when I'm with Brian we talk business or sports."

She smiled. "That's the way most men are, I guess."

His blue eyes were intense. "Do you know the way men are?"

"I've dated a few." She kept her tone light.

Glancing at the pictures on the wall, he studied his ancestors for a few moments, then put one hand on her shoulder and looked directly into her eyes. "I'd like you to answer a question."

"What?" She hoped her voice didn't sound as trembly as she felt inside.

"*Are* you attracted to Brian? Do you wish there was more between you than a professional relationship...than a big brother relationship?"

"I've never, *ever* looked at Brian in that way," she replied without hesitation.

Now his free hand lightly capped her other shoulder and he drew her a little closer. "So we're left with us. Am I crazy or does the earth move a little bit each time we're together?"

She could end this right here and now. She could say her earth was stable and nothing he said or did affected it. But she had to be honest with him, at least about this.

"It does—but you're Brian's friend and older than I am. We're working together, and the truth is, I don't want to get involved with anyone right now."

"Because…"

"Because of where I want to go and what I want to do and who I want to be."

"Your career means everything to you."

This time she *did* hesitate. "Not everything, but it's the main focus of my life right now. It just has to be. Besides that—" She stopped, then went on. "When I get involved with a man, I don't ever want to be like a trinket he picks up and then eventually throws away."

There was a flicker of emotion in Alan's eyes. He slid one hand from her shoulder to the locket dangling between her open lapels. "You want to be treasured the way you treasure this."

She nodded, but couldn't speak. That was probably her most secret dream. She kept telling herself it might happen in the future if she ever achieved all her goals. Her throat was tight and Alan's hand on the locket made her uneasy and anxious and happy and scared, all at the same time. What would he say if she told him about Timothy?

When he let the locket slip from his fingers, she knew he'd really listened to what she'd said. But when his thumb traced the outline of her lips, when he looked at her as if kissing her was the only thing on his mind, she wasn't sure about the present or the future or her plans or the next step.

"We'd better go to lunch or Maude's going to send out a search party." His voice was slightly husky, and Lisa knew he was thinking about the kisses they could share, and maybe more.

"Lunch," she agreed, though she'd forgotten all about it as she'd gazed into Alan's eyes. Maybe as she ate, she could put everything into perspective. She could forget her longing to be held in Alan Barrett's arms.

Maybe she was being naive for her twenty-one years and she'd better grow up.

Fast.

Chapter Five

"Why don't you take Miss Sanders out to the barn," Maude suggested to Alan after the mid-afternoon lunch, "and show her that calf Christina's been helping the foreman to nurse."

"Please call me Lisa." Lisa already liked Maude and felt only approval from the grandmotherly house-keeper. Approval was more important to her now than it used to be—especially Alan's approval. She was pleased that Maude was willing to include her in the happenings on the ranch.

"Lisa might not want anything to do with the calf." Alan seemed to be giving her an out if she wanted it.

"I've never been around cows, but I *do* like animals," she assured them both. "Do you feed it with a bottle?"

"Sure do." Maude took one from the refrigerator and warmed it under the hot spigot.

"Do you want to come along?" Alan asked Brian with a grin.

"I think I'll pass. There are some properties I want to research on the Internet and some calls I need to make. You two go ahead."

Lisa and Alan didn't speak as they crossed to the barn, though she sneaked peeks at him as they walked. He had a loose athletic gait that had her almost running to keep up. Though he'd captured her attention, she couldn't help taking in everything about her new surroundings—the firs in the distance, the shady cottonwoods, the golden fields absolutely everywhere. There were scents of leaves and pine needles and animals and fresh cold air.

When they passed through the corral gate, Lisa saw a black horse with a white forelock poke its head out of a stall. She smiled. But as soon as she thought about her one other encounter with horses, her smile faded.

After Timothy had been kidnapped by the black market baby ring soon after he was born, she and Brian and Carrie had spent days and nights sitting by the phone, creating flyers, constantly checking with the police department and the FBI. It had been an awful time. One afternoon Brian had convinced her and Carrie to go with him to a friend's house, horseback riding. That day Lisa had hardly known what she was doing. Her thoughts had been elsewhere—with the baby who was no longer hers, wondering what was happening to him, where the kidnapper might be holding him. She'd still been connected to him. Whenever she thought about that awful time, she tried to focus on the day Timothy was found—the moment he'd been returned to Carrie's arms—rather than the rest of it.

Why was she thinking about this now? Because she'd met a man who awakened dreams again? She told herself she didn't deserve those dreams, at least not yet.

The immense building sat on a hill. They entered the bottom portion, which was devoted to the animals. When she stepped into the barn, Lisa felt she was entering a foreign land. As Alan took her elbow and pointed to the stall housing the calf, she guessed sometimes romantic dreams didn't—couldn't—wait. Still…when she fell in love, she wanted it to be forever. How could Alan be interested in her when he didn't really know anything about her? Not the things that mattered, anyway.

A man like him, who could have any woman in the world…

She could feel the heat of his fingers through her denim jacket. When she looked up at him, she thought about the fairy tales her mom had read to her when Lisa's world had been normal and safe.

"Christina named the calf Chocolate Ripple because of her color. She calls her Choco for short."

The calf brayed and stared at Lisa with big, liquid brown eyes.

"She's adorable!"

"Maybe," Alan agreed with a wry expression. "But as

I have to remind Christina, she's *not* a pet. We're just taking care of her like her momma would until she can go out and run with the other calves." He handed Lisa the bottle. "Do you want to try it?"

"Sure."

Alan opened the door to the stall and they stepped inside. The smell of hay and animals was strong, but Lisa realized she liked the earthiness of it. The calf eyed Lisa and stood perfectly still while she came closer.

"Hi there, baby," Lisa crooned. "Do you want some of this?"

Lisa had no sooner held up the bottle than the calf latched on to it and started drinking enthusiastically. Lisa laughed and petted her. "I don't know, Alan. If your daughter's taking care of her, she might become attached."

"She can't take her along to college."

"No, I guess not." Lisa continued stroking the animal while the calf sucked.

"Why weren't you afraid of her?" Alan asked, an interested expression on his face.

Lisa glanced over at him. He was leaning against the railing, elbows hitched over the top plank, assessing her.

"Why *would* I be afraid? Just look at her."

"Cows can be ornery."

"So can people."

At that, Alan straightened, taking a step closer. "That's one way of looking at the world, I guess."

"How do *you* look at it?" She wanted to know so much about him.

"Until somebody steps on my toes, I give them a chance."

Since her parents died, she'd become defensive and mistrustful. Even now she trusted only Carrie and Brian and a couple of close friends. On the streets she'd had to rely on her instincts. "I try to *prevent* somebody from stepping on my toes."

"And just how do you do that?"

"I've developed a kind of radar. I don't take much on face value and I go by the vibes I feel underneath."

As the calf finished with the bottle, Lisa put her arm around her neck and petted her. "Don't you go on instinct to know who to do business with or not?"

"I suppose I do. I never thought about it like that."

Lisa remembered the vibes she'd gotten from Brian the first time she'd met him. He'd disapproved of everything about her. Yet because of Carrie, he'd given her a chance, and Lisa had come to realize he might be a bit rigid at times and not always open to new and different things, but when he cared, he cared. She was getting the feeling that Alan's bonds were deep and strong, too, especially those with his daughter, his brother and with Maude.

"I bet it's hard for you to leave the Lazy B when you fly off to make deals."

"You bet right. My life is here."

"Did you live here when you were married?" She knew the question was personal, but she couldn't learn anything about him if she didn't ask.

A closed look swept across Alan's face, but then he nodded. "Yes, we lived here."

Suddenly there were years of experience in Alan's eyes—experience of things she'd never know. He'd been married for ten years. He'd raised a daughter. He'd flown around the country, becoming familiar with places she'd probably only dream of seeing. Yet she sensed deep-down kindness in him. More than that, she felt the sharp edge of an attraction she'd never known before. It was more elemental than picking a guy with a great smile and a terrific body. It was scorching and stirring and down-right terrifying when she admitted it was there.

They were attracted to each other. But could there be more?

She shivered. She'd left the house so quickly, she hadn't picked up her coat. Her mind had been on Alan, not the colder Texas weather. As she shivered again, Alan noticed.

"Come on," he said, leading her out of the stall. "Before I give you any more of the tour, you need to get warm."

She followed him into the tack room, where he took a plaid flannel jacket from a hook. "I keep this out here. Sometimes I come out to the barn intending to spend only a few minutes, and end up staying longer."

He held it for her as she slipped first one arm in and then the other. It smelled of saddle leather and of men's aftershave, the same scent that Alan was wearing.

The collar caught under her hair, and he straightened it, his fingers sliding through her locks in the process. "It's mighty big, but it will do."

She felt warmer already. But that probably wasn't because of the flannel jacket so much as standing close to Alan, looking up at his craggy face, staring into his too blue eyes.

"Damn it, Lisa, don't look at me like that," he practically growled.

"Like what?"

"Like you're as curious about me as I am about you."

"Curious?" she asked, her voice thready.

"You know those vibes you were talking about?"

She nodded.

"I'm feeling them from you. Vibes that are telling me to do one thing while I know damn well I should do another. If you were a few years older—"

She cut him off angrily. "And exactly what difference would a few years make? You're acting as if I don't know the score. I'm twenty-one, I can vote, drink and kiss any man I want."

His hands rested on her shoulders now. "A kiss could start something neither of us are ready for."

"Or it could prove there's nothing for either of us to worry about. You know—all smoke and no fire."

"Lisa." Her name was a protest…a warning.

She could back away now while she still had the chance.

But she didn't want to back away. She wanted to feel Alan's lips on hers. She wanted to experience his kiss and discover whether the excitement between them was real or imagined, something fleeting or something that could last.

From the moment Alan's lips brushed against hers, her

whole body tingled. *More* was all she could think of—more of the exquisite sensations, more of inhaling Alan's scent, more of experiencing a real kiss for the first time in her life. Oh, sure, she'd been kissed before. But she'd never felt like this, never felt as if she were going to explode, never felt as if this man had the power to propel her into a universe she'd never known. Maybe that was the crux of it. In the past she'd only kissed *boys*.

She could tell he was holding back and giving her plenty of chances to back away. She wasn't going anywhere. Her tongue touched the seam of his lips and he groaned, wrapping his arms around her. It was odd, but in the midst of the maelstrom of erotic sensations, in the midst of his tongue tasting hers, she felt safe and pro-tected within the circle of his strong arms. No matter what happened, he wouldn't let her fall or get lost or drown in something she didn't understand.

He delved into her mouth, exploring, and she explored him. She tasted the faint trace of coffee he'd had with lunch. When his hands passed up and down her back, pulling her closer, she pushed into him, having forgotten what man-and-woman contact felt like. It had been so long since she'd been with Thad, so long since she'd let a man get this close. Thad had been a boy, intent on pleasure. Alan…Alan was intent on *giving* her pleasure, as well as taking his. He was on a mission of discovery, as was she, and the give and take was equal. As his belt buckle pressed into her stomach, she felt the hardness of him, the arousal that gave her power and confidence as a woman.

The sound of the barn door opening broke the moment. Female voices lifted to the rafters and floated down the walkway between the stalls.

Alan responded first, breaking away from her, swearing, muttering something like "old enough to know better." Then he used his shirt cuff to rub lipstick from his lips, and in the next moment was smoothing smeared lipstick from below hers.

His thumb traced under her bottom lip again. "That'll have to do."

He called out the door of the tack room. "We're in here." Obviously, he'd recognized the voices.

A moment later, a tall redhead about Alan's age stood in the doorway, next to a striking teenager whose hair was more brown than red, curly and shoulder length. Freckles ran across her nose and cheeks, and her blue eyes were almost as spellbinding as Alan's.

The woman examined Lisa quickly but thoroughly, then glanced at Alan. "Maude said you were out here."

Christina was in Alan's arms, hugging him. "It seems like forever since I've seen you."

"It's been less than two weeks." He grinned, hugging her back. "It's not as if I don't talk to you almost every day."

His daughter released him and wrinkled her nose. "I know. I guess in the fall I'll have to make the most of talking to you, because it will definitely be a while between visits."

"And why is that?"

"Because I decided to go to the University of Illinois."

"That means animal sciences rather than premed?"

Christina nodded her head and his ex-wife just looked unhappy.

Feeling as if she'd fallen into the midst of a family dispute, Lisa wanted to slide away and make her exit. There was no way to gracefully do that.

"We can discuss this later," Alan said. "Let me introduce you to...a colleague. Lisa Sanders, meet my daughter, Christina, and her mother, Sherri."

Lisa extended her hand to the ex-wife.

Sherri shook it quickly. "A colleague?"

"I work with Summers Development in Portland." Lisa turned to Christina. When she extended her hand, Alan's daughter smiled at her and squeezed it more than shook it.

She seemed to appraise Lisa with interest and then she grinned. "Are you working on the golf resort?"

Apparently Christina kept up with what her father was doing. "Yes, I am. Today your dad is giving me a tour of the ranch. And I fed Choco."

"Isn't she just too adorable? Dad says I can't make her a pet, but maybe I can convince him otherwise."

"Oh, no, you don't," Alan warned her. "Don't even think you're going to get Lisa on your side."

"I think she's adorable, too," Lisa said in an aside to his daughter. "Maybe she can be a mascot for one of the horses and stay in the barn."

"That calf is not a goat or a dog," Alan protested firmly.

When Lisa and Christina laughed, he shook his head. "Oh, great. *Two* of you pulling my leg."

"We can't stay," Sherri said stiffly. "Christina and I are going shopping for a dress for the Valentine's Day dance at school. Since we can't go tomorrow," she added.

"Are we still going to look for a car tomorrow?" Christina asked Alan.

"We sure are. If your mom brings you out again after school, we'll have the rest of the evening. Are you coming along?" he asked Sherri.

"No. I have a community theater meeting tomorrow night. Besides, it's a father-daughter thing. You two would outvote me, anyway. I'm going to go get that recipe for a taco casserole from Maude. I'll meet you at the car in about fifteen minutes, honey, okay?"

"Sure, Mom."

Sherri gave Alan and Lisa one last look, then turned and left.

Christina fairly ran to the calf's stall. "I want to spend a few minutes with Choco. Lisa, why don't you come with me? You can tell me where you're from and how you got into real estate."

Lisa wasn't sure exactly what she should do, but Christina seemed to want to talk to her, so she followed her down the walkway. She could feel Alan's gaze on her. Soon, however, they were inside the stall, cooing over the calf, and Alan had gone to the tack room.

Lowering her voice, Christina asked, "Were you and Dad making out before Mom and I came in?"

Caught off guard, Lisa was at a total loss for words.

"It's okay. Mom probably didn't notice. But Dad has

lipstick on his cuff and you've got a smear above your lip—just a little one."

This conversation could go one of two ways, depending on Christina. Cautiously Lisa replied, "Your dad and I just met a week ago."

"I saw the way he looks at you. He likes you!"

"Christina, I'm not sure we should be discussing this."

Alan's daughter looked her straight in the eye. "It's okay, you know, if you and Dad have a thing going. In fact, I think it's cool. He needs someone to shake up his world a little."

When Lisa glanced down the walkway, she saw Alan was still moving around in the tack room. "I'm sure he dates."

"Not seriously."

Something must have shown in Lisa's expression.

"Oh, I don't mean he doesn't *want* to date seriously, but nothing seems to work out. It's like he picks women who don't like the same things he does or don't care about ranches or don't like animals."

"You think he sabotages himself?"

"I don't know if it's that. Maybe the only women he's around are his age, professional, set in their ways."

"You notice a lot."

"He's my dad."

Yes, he was, and Lisa had to be extra careful what she said and what she did. "Your dad and I hardly know each other, Christina."

The teenager scratched Choco between the ears. "But you were kissing."

Lisa felt her face go pink and admitted, "It was the first time, so please don't get the idea that something's going on when it isn't."

Alan's daughter gave her that smile again. "You're from Portland?"

"Yes, I am."

"Dad bought a condo so he could spend more time there. If you're working on this deal together, you'll probably be seeing a lot of each other."

"I'm not his equal. I mean," she hurriedly explained, "I'm Brian Summers's assistant, so I'm acting as Alan's assistant, too. That's all."

A car horn beeped twice.

"That's Mom." Christina sighed with a roll of her eyes. "She wants to do this mother-daughter bonding thing over finding a dress. I already know which one I want. I just have to point her in the right direction and convince her it's right for me."

Lisa smiled. Christina obviously knew her parents well and played them when she could. "Do you already know what kind of car you want, too?"

"I'm open to suggestions on that, and I know Dad will have a few. You'll be here tomorrow night, right?"

"I think we're going to be here a few days."

"Great. Why don't you come along with Dad and me?"

"Oh, I don't know…"

"Hey, Dad," Christina yelled into the tack room.

Alan came out with a saddle in his arms. "Are you leaving?"

"Yeah, but I want Lisa to come along tomorrow night when we look at cars. Can she?"

If Alan was surprised, he didn't show it. "I suppose she can." He glanced at Lisa. "Do you know anything about cars?"

It just so happened that she did. "A friend of mine owns a motorcycle shop. I've watched him work. He likes to tinker with cars, too, so I've learned a few things."

Looking impressed, Christina responded, "See, Dad? She'll be an asset!" The teenager put her hand on Lisa's arm. "Please come. Don't think you're horning in, because you're not. It will help me to have another opinion."

Before Lisa could respond, Christina was hugging her father again, then flying out the door.

The silence in the barn seemed to pound in Lisa's ears.

"Let's go for a ride," Alan suggested.

Lisa quickly swiveled around to look at him. "A ride?"

"I'll saddle up two horses. Blue Bonnet's gentle. You'll like her."

That was the last thing she'd expected, out of all the things he could have said. "We should talk."

"No. Let's give everything time to settle, then we'll talk."

"Won't Brian wonder where we are?"

Hoisting the saddle onto the top plank of the stall, he took his cell phone from his pocket and pressed a button. "I'll call over to Maude. She'll let him know. When he's making business calls, he forgets about everything else. He won't miss us for a little while."

Lisa wasn't so sure about that. Yes, when Brian got engrossed in business, he had tunnel vision. But he didn't miss much of anything. She knew that from experience. Still, climbing onto a horse and actually riding with Alan would be unforgettable, something she could tuck away in her closet of memories.

"I'd like to go riding. Don't you need a coat?"

"There's a closet in the tack room. I'll find something for both of us." He nodded to the jacket he'd given her. "That won't be enough if the wind picks up."

Fifteen minutes later, Lisa was wearing someone's down jacket. It was way too big for her. Alan had found a sweatshirt for himself and buttoned an insulated vest on top. He'd also given Lisa a hat that was as hard as a helmet, with a chin strap. She felt a bit foolish wearing it.

"You're sure I need this?" she asked him as he stood beside her, ready to help her up onto the horse.

"You haven't had much experience riding. Better to be safe than sorry. Come on, put your foot in my hands and I'll give you a boost up, then I'll adjust your stirrups."

She looked at him as if he'd lost his mind. "I can't just step into your hands—"

"Sure, you can. Hold on to the pommel and I'll have you in the saddle before you know it. Unless you want me to pick you up and put you there myself."

"I don't think that would be a good idea." She could still feel the reverberations from their kiss whenever she thought about it.

"Come on then," he coaxed with a grin.

Feeling foolish, she took hold of the saddle horn and

put her foot into his hands. Seconds later, she was atop Blue Bonnet, looking down at a man who could make her heart gallop without even trying.

"I like your daughter," she said simply.

"I think she liked you. She wouldn't have invited you to come along tomorrow night if she hadn't."

"But I don't have to go if that makes you uncomfortable—"

"Makes *me* uncomfortable? I've been uncomfortable since the minute I set eyes on you."

"Then why did you ask me to go riding?" *He* had kissed her, although she'd kissed him back. *He* was the one who had followed her to her apartment. *He* had come to her interview with Carrie. "If I make you so uncomfortable, maybe I should just go back to the house and help Brian with his calls. I'm sure there's *something* I can do."

Alan's hand was on her leg, as if that would keep her in the saddle. "Whoa, there. That didn't come out right. Lisa, I sure as shooting don't know what to do about you. That kiss confirmed my worst suspicions. We're dynamite together. How are we going to work together with that between us?"

"I can be professional. I can put it out of my mind."

He raised his brows.

"We're adults, Alan. We can do anything we have to."

"I feel a hell of a lot more adult than you are."

"Will you stop with the age thing? Whether you're twenty-eight or thirty-eight or fifty-eight, I don't want to get involved any more than *you* do."

"You'd date a man who's fifty-eight?"

She breathed out a sigh of frustration. "No. I know we're in different places in our lives. I know you probably just want to have a good time with women. No strings."

"Did I say that?"

"No, but you've been divorced for seven years and haven't gotten serious with anyone."

"And how do you know that?"

"Christina told me."

"In a five minute conversation?" He seemed genuinely unnerved.

"It…came up."

Taking his hand from her leg, he shook his head. "That's it. We're going for that ride. No more talking. No more discussing. No more kissing. We'll get some perspective if we have to ride from here into the next county."

After that pronouncement, he mounted his horse and turned the gelding toward the open corral gate.

Lisa followed him, convinced a ride from here all the way to Portland wouldn't give them perspective. His kiss had moved her like she'd never been moved before. If her kiss had done anywhere near that to him, then neither of them would be able to think straight if it happened again.

If it happened again.

They hadn't discussed anything, nor had they cleared their heads. At least that was Alan's estimation of their ride. Lisa might not have had much experience on horses, but she was a natural rider. He hadn't had to give her much instruction.

He'd loved watching her as she caught a glimpse of things she'd never seen before, as she'd felt the exhilaration of being on the back of a horse, the wind moving by her. She hadn't wanted to simply walk or even trot. She'd wanted to go faster. He'd been unsure about letting her at first, but then he'd given her the go-ahead and he'd watched as she'd raced across the meadow.

She was going to be sore in the morning.

At the corral, one of the hands would have taken the horses, but Alan asked Lisa, "Do you want to go up to the house or do you want to help me groom them?"

"I'd like to help groom them. Just tell me what to do."

Her enthusiasm was one of the things about her that got to him. She was almost fearless, and he wondered if that came with her youth. Yet he had the feeling part of her had always been, and would always *be* fearless.

"I can attach Blue in the walkway if you don't want to be confined in her stall with her."

"She'll probably be more at home in her stall. I know to stay away from her feet."

Yep, fearless *and* in tune with animals, from what he could see.

When he handed Lisa the grooming brush, even though the stall gate separated them, their fingers touched, and all the memories and sensations from their kiss came rushing back. He quickly entered his horse's stall and began the rubdown process.

Twenty minutes later, they were both finished and putting away the brushes in the tack room. Lisa took off the coat he had given her to wear, and he stowed it in the closet. All of a sudden he heard a small cry, and then saw distress on her face.

"What's wrong?"

"My locket. It's not around my neck. I can't lose it."

He took her by the arm. "Hold on, we'll find it."

"But what if I lost it while I was riding?"

"And what if you didn't? Come on. Look around and then check Blue's stall."

A search of the barn where they'd come and gone provided no clue. The shiny gold necklace didn't twinkle up at them. Alan could see Lisa was upset. That locket meant the world to her and he wanted to know why. Just because it was an antique? Because Carrie had given it to her?

He took Blue out of her stall once more and tied her in the walkway. Then he took a pitchfork and carefully sifted through the hay, realizing how easily the chain could get caught up in it. This was worse than searching for a needle in a haystack.

All at once, Lisa pointed to a corner of the stall. "There. I think I see something. A flash of gold."

He couldn't see a damn thing. He tried feeling instead of looking, and his fingers brushed a smooth, hard object. Grasping it, he saw her locket nestled in his hand.

"I've got it." He felt jubilant, as if he should win some great prize.

But Lisa didn't look relieved. She looked…scared.

Quickly she snatched it from his hand. "Thank you. This really means a lot to me. I'm going to take it up to the house and make sure it doesn't happen again." Then she was leaving the barn with her secrets, and Alan wondered if he'd ever learn what they were.

As he led Blue back into her stall, the barn door opened and shut again. Maybe Lisa had returned?

But when he looked over the horse's rump, he saw Brian coming toward him, and his expression was very serious.

"I think we should have a talk."

"About the phone calls you made?" Maybe Brian had run into trouble with some of the investors. Money could be pulled out as easily as promised.

"No, I want to talk to you about Lisa."

Alan guessed he knew what was coming. He also guessed he wasn't going to like it.

Chapter Six

"What did you say to Lisa to upset her?" Brian demanded, hands on his hips, shirtsleeves rolled up his forearms, his tie pulled to one side.

"I didn't say *anything* to upset her," Alan replied defensively. "After Christina and Sherri left, Lisa and I went for a ride. We groomed the horses and she realized she'd lost her locket."

"Lost her locket?" Brian looked concerned.

"We found it again, but afterward she took off for the house."

Brian's silence was almost as unsettling as his question had been.

"I know that locket's important to her," Alan

prompted, "because Carrie gave it to her. Maybe she can have a heavier chain put on it."

"I'm sure she'll do that. Look, Alan, there's something I have to ask you. I look on Lisa as if she were a…a niece, and I don't want her to get into a situation with you that she can't handle."

"Do you regret bringing her along?"

"Not yet I don't, but I soon will if what I suspect is true. Is something going on between the two of you?"

Alan didn't like being given the third degree, but in the situation they were in, Brian had every right to ask questions. He seemed to see himself in the role of Lisa's protector, and Alan wondered exactly how he'd come to be that.

"I'm attracted to her and she's attracted to me. But it's more than that, too. I like being around her. She's fresh and blunt and doesn't take any flack from me. But I get the feeling she doesn't trust easily. Am I right about that?"

"You'll have to talk to her about trust. But I will tell you she's vulnerable. She's young and she's just starting to build her future. Don't mess with her without good reason, without some strong feelings behind it or without awfully good intentions."

"For all that bravado, she's not experienced, is she?" Alan was too curious *not* to ask.

Brian's cheeks flushed. "That's not a question for me to answer. Tell me something, why are you even looking at Lisa when you can have almost any woman you want?"

"That's the thing, Brian." He still didn't understand what had happened himself. "In the past couple of years, one-night stands and get-away weekends just don't cut it anymore. I find myself restless, but not wanting to go out. I don't want to get into the same conversations about my work. I don't want to go to bed with a woman and then in the morning still feel…empty. So I quit doing it. I quit *wanting* to do it. But when I met Lisa… There's something about her that intrigues me. For all the reasons you've stated, I've told myself to stay far away from her."

"Are you going to do that?"

Alan ran his hand over his face, then stuffed it into his pocket. "I was just going to concentrate on business, but Christina asked Lisa to go along car shopping with us tomorrow night."

"They hit it off?"

"It seems like it. Hell, they're close to the same age."

"Not exactly. There's a big difference between seventeen and twenty-one. Lisa hasn't been as—" He stopped abruptly.

"Hasn't been as what? Finish what you were going to say."

Brian let out a sigh. "Lisa hasn't been as sheltered as Christina. She had to grow up fast after her parents died."

"She told me her aunt didn't want her. Is that true?"

"Yes."

"But she really wasn't clear about why she came back to Portland and teamed up with you and Carrie."

"That's her story to tell."

"You want me to be patient," Alan muttered, frustrated that he couldn't get more information from Brian.

"I'm not sure I want you to be anything where Lisa's concerned. You're seventeen years older!"

"Yeah, I know. That fact hasn't escaped me. And it hasn't escaped Lisa, either. She's already informed me she doesn't want to get involved with *anyone,* so all of this might be moot."

He could only hope that his fascination with Lisa was a passing fancy. Tomorrow morning he'd wake up and it would be over. He could go on his way as if he'd never met her.

Fat chance.

When Sherri dropped off Christina the following afternoon, Alan knew there was trouble.

Christina came into the kitchen and warned him, "Mom wants to talk to you."

Peering out the window, Alan could see Sherri was still sitting in her car. "Then why didn't she come in?"

"She's on her way somewhere and didn't want to bother getting out."

That didn't sound like Sherri. She never hesitated to come into the house. But then his gaze fell on Lisa, who was already talking to his daughter about what dealerships she wanted to go to.

He had to admit, he'd been surprised by Lisa today. She had related both to the investors they'd showed properties to as well as to the agents showing the properties. She already had a surprisingly good knowledge of the financial determinates, as well as the property values.

She'd stayed in the background while he and Brian had talked about the development of the golf resort, but she was well versed on subjects ranging from the benefits of walking eighteen holes to what products a pro shop should carry. She'd done her research. Besides that, everyone she talked to just seemed to relate to her.

Except…he and Lisa had *not* related today. They'd kept their distance. Since his talk with Brian, he was sure there were too many obstacles between them.

That was solid reasoning, yet it didn't sit well with him. Not well at all.

As he strode to Sherri's sedan and put his hand on the roof of her car, she looked up at him with a frown he'd seen often in the last years of their marriage.

"Do you think it's proper to take this Lisa Sanders along to the dealerships?"

"I don't think 'proper' has anything to do with it. Christina asked her to go along. Didn't she tell you that?"

"She told me, but I wondered if she had some prodding."

Attempting to keep the lid on his temper, he managed to say evenly, "Christina liked Lisa, but I think she believes Lisa will be on her side if she and I disagree."

"And just what does it matter what Ms. Sanders thinks?"

"Sherri, don't make a mountain out of this."

"I'm not making a mountain out of it. I'm just asking a few questions. Is she your latest cuddle-bunny?"

"She is *not*."

"You're going to tell me your association with her is strictly professional?"

He'd never lied to Sherri and he wouldn't start now. "I've got to admit, she's a bit intriguing."

"Intriguing? Are you having a midlife crisis? She's young enough to be your daughter!"

"Lisa is twenty-one. I would have had to have been seventeen when I fathered her."

"Which is not an impossibility."

The silence between them was filled with the vibrations that had characterized so much of their marriage. "I'm not going to get into an argument about this. Christina wanted her to come along and I didn't see any harm in it. Other than that, I don't think it's any of your business."

"What affects our daughter is my business."

"Do you want to take Christina car shopping? I can just turn the whole situation over to you."

Sherri looked as if she was honestly considering it, then shook her head. "No, Christina would never forgive me. She wanted to do this with you. Just don't let her get anything too big or too powerful or too low to the ground, or one of those SUVs that can roll over."

"You've just eliminated most of the cars being sold now." He'd always tried humor with Sherri, but it had never taken very well. It didn't now, either.

She sighed. "You'll let her do whatever she wants. I just know you will."

"I'll make sure she buys a car with a suitable number of air bags and safety features."

"Promise?"

"I promise."

After another sigh, she shifted her car into gear. "I wish she was four again."

Alan knew exactly what his ex-wife meant. In some ways he did, too. But Christina was developing into a beautiful, wonderful, intelligent woman, and he couldn't wait to see what she'd accomplish. As he watched Sherri drive away, he knew their marriage had been a mistake…but having Christina hadn't been. She was a blessing he'd always be thankful for.

"She likes the yellow one," Lisa said to Alan as they watched Christina run her hand over the hood of the small sporty car.

"You do, too. I can tell."

When Lisa's gaze met his, he could see she was surprised by his observation. "Well, don't you?" he repeated.

"I was trying to remain impartial."

He gave a wry laugh. "You can't hide excitement, and that sparkle in your eyes goes along with liking a car a whole lot."

"*You* don't like it?"

"Her *mother's* not going to like it. It has a good safety rating for a car that size, but Sherri will think it's too sporty, too fast, too small."

"It's the one Christina wants," Lisa assured him.

"Yeah, and that's part of it, too. *Should* I get her what she wants? Maybe we should have gone to the used dealership. Maybe I should require her to pay me something out of every check she earns this summer. You'd think this parenting thing would get easier after seventeen years."

"Being a parent has got to be the hardest job in the world."

"It's certainly the most baffling. Maybe a boy would have been simpler."

"And if you'd had a boy, you might have thought a girl would have been simpler."

"All I know is, when she drives off in that car, I'll wish *I* was still driving her," he grumbled.

"You can't put her in a protective bubble, Alan. She has to make her own decisions and choices and mistakes."

They were both wearing jackets, but he swore he could feel heat as their elbows brushed. "How did you get so smart?"

"I'm not smart. I just made my share of mistakes."

He knew if he asked her what those mistakes were, she wouldn't tell him. She would become evasive or change the subject. Because she didn't trust him? Or because she wanted to trust him, yet was afraid to?

Although they were standing in the middle of the car lot with bright shiny vehicles all around, his daughter about fifteen yards away, Alan looked into Lisa's big green eyes and just wanted to wrap her in his arms. When he'd held her in the barn, she'd felt so good. Oh, yeah, physically she'd turned him on in ways he hadn't been turned on in years. But his reaction hadn't been just physical, and he didn't think he was deluding himself about that.

Was he having a midlife crisis?

After the salesman finished showing Christina the intricacies of the car, she came over to Alan, grinning from ear to ear. "I really like that one, Dad. Really, really. And it even has OnStar, which should give you some sense of security about it. If I'm in an accident and my air bag goes off, they'll send emergency services."

"The other cars we drove had it, too."

"Yeah, I know, but they weren't yellow and this one's great on gas. What do you think?"

He thought he was a father with an almost perfect daughter whom he'd loved dearly from the moment she was born. "I think if that's the car you want, then that's the car we'll buy."

She threw her arms around his neck and gave him a huge hug.

Over his daughter's shoulder, Alan caught sight of Lisa watching them. He could have sworn he saw her wipe a tear from her eye.

I can't be falling for him, Lisa scolded herself with dismay as she sat beside Alan in his SUV, heading toward the ranch. He had a daughter who was obviously the light of his life. He'd quit college to take on the responsibility of being a husband and a father. He'd never understand that she'd given up her baby to go to college, to make a life different from the one she'd known on the streets. He'd just *never* understand.

When she was eighteen, she'd made the only decision

she thought she could make, the one that was right for her baby. How could she have provided food and shelter, as well as paid for doctors' visits? How could her baby have had a future with her low-paying jobs? Still, looking back at it now, she wondered if she'd just been selfish…if she'd taken the easy way out.

Giving up a child isn't the easy way out. But even as her heart told her that, she still felt guilty.

"She should be home by now," Alan said.

"You couldn't follow her. She'd think you don't trust her."

Alan's cell phone chirped and he slipped it from his jacket pocket.

When Lisa saw his smile, she knew Christina had arrived home safely.

He didn't talk long. After he closed the phone and slid it back into his pocket, he said, "She's not sure her mom likes it, but *she* certainly does."

Suddenly he turned off the road into a convenience store parking lot. "I told Maude I'd pick up a dozen eggs. She's afraid she'll run out for breakfast."

"And I can use some nail polish remover. I forgot mine when I packed."

In the glow of the dash lights, his gaze went to Lisa's hands. She'd polished her nails yesterday before they'd left, a light mauve that would go with all the clothes she'd brought along. But one was already chipped, and that wouldn't do, with meeting clients again tomorrow.

Reaching out, he covered her hand with his. "Thanks

for coming along tonight. It meant a lot to Christina. Sometimes she doesn't trust my opinion or her mother's."

"It was fun. I've never test driven new cars before."

"Yours wasn't new when you bought it?"

Uh-oh, dangerous territory. She should just keep her mouth shut when she was with Alan, so she wouldn't get into trouble or reveal too much. She'd saved money ever since she'd started working, because she'd known she would need a car when she graduated. As a graduation present, however, Brian and Carrie had given her money to add to her savings for a down payment. She never could have afforded a new one.

"Brian helped me pick out a good used car."

"That's the first car you've ever owned?"

She nodded. "Not every teenager can have a car of her own, Alan."

"No, I suppose not. I guess I took for granted the way I was raised, and Christina does, too." His hand still holding Lisa's, he asked, "But *you* don't take anything for granted, do you?"

The tingles that were shooting up her arm were electric. Her pulse seemed to be pounding in her ears. Who would have thought holding hands with a man could be so…so exciting? Yet he'd asked her something very serious and she had to answer him.

"No, I don't take much for granted," she responded. "Maybe that's because one day I had a great life, two parents who loved me, and the next I didn't."

After a long pause, he admitted, "When my mother

died, we were all devastated. But Neal and I had each other and Dad. Our lives basically didn't change."

Alan and Lisa were leaning toward each other now. It just seemed natural. How could they have so many differences between them, yet she could still feel connected to him? She couldn't know a man in a week and he couldn't know her.

A pickup truck veered into the parking lot, its headlights glaring into Alan's SUV. He released her hand. "Come on, let's get what we need and head back to the ranch, or Brian will send out the calvary."

Lisa wondered what *that* meant.

In the convenience store, she and Alan went their separate ways. He crossed to the refrigerated cases, while she found the cosmetics aisle. Five minutes later, nail polish remover, makeup swabs, a magazine and her favorite chocolate candy bar in hand, she found Alan talking to a short, husky man by the milk case.

"All set," she said with a smile.

Alan was holding the dozen eggs. "I got sidetracked. I hadn't seen Fred for a while. Fred Gordon, this is Lisa Sanders."

Fred's ten-gallon hat seemed way too big for his head. He shook her hand. "Good to meet you. Are you a friend of Christina's?"

Lisa saw the expression on Alan's face. Fred Gordon had jumped to the conclusion that she was young enough to belong with Christina's group of friends, and Alan might be taxiing her around.

She didn't want to embarrass the man, yet she didn't know what Alan would want her to say, either. So she merely replied, "I'm visiting from Portland."

"Kids these days surely get around. I didn't leave the county till I was thirty. Well, it was good seeing you, Alan. Don't be a stranger. Just because Neal buys a horse from me now and then, doesn't mean you can't, too."

"I'll remember that," Alan answered with a smile that didn't reach his eyes.

When Fred Gordon had walked away, Lisa lowered her voice. "I didn't know what to say."

"You handled it nicely." Alan's tone was cool and polite and held none of the warmth she'd felt from him when they'd been sitting in the car holding hands. She supposed the reality of the situation had hit him with his friend's comment. If he cared what other people thought…

Did *she* care what other people thought? She never had in the past. But she realized that wasn't true anymore. She cared what Brian and Carrie thought. She cared what Alan thought.

Her heart hurt because she never wanted to tell him about the mistake she'd made and how selfish she'd been.

At midnight, Lisa still wasn't asleep. She stood on her balcony, watching a light snow falling. She smiled at the sight—it hardly ever snowed in Portland. A few flakes blew here and there, swirling around, and she shivered because she'd come outside in her robe.

Restless and needing space beyond her balcony, she

went into her room, put on jeans, a sweater and sneakers, and grabbed her leather jacket. The house was silent. Night-lights glowed here and there, illuminating her way. She slipped out a sliding glass door in the dining room and found herself on the brick patio.

Beyond the fenced-in pool stood a five-sided pool house nestled against an even higher privacy fence. In the other corner stood a hot tub. Walking along the length of the rectangular pool, she lifted her face up to the snowflakes, and one fell on her nose. She was getting chilled. The cedar-sided pool house drew her attention and she went toward it, thinking it was big enough to be a guest house. She really didn't expect the door to be open, but when she turned the knob, it was. Flicking a light switch by the door, she found the space illuminated by a table lamp.

There was a partition dividing the equipment part of the pool house from the sitting area. In the latter was a cast-iron stove. From the controls, Lisa figured it was fueled by gas. Across from it sat a leather love seat and club chair in a beautiful shade of teal. The wrought-iron table held a Tiffany lamp.

Crossing to the stove, Lisa could see the pilot was lit. She pressed the starter button and the stove came to life, the fire burning behind the ceramic logs. The chill diminished and she opened her jacket and slipped it off. Then she sat on the love seat and watched the snow fall through the glass window in the door.

Suddenly she wasn't just looking at the snow, but at a

tall figure of a man. Her breath caught until she realized it was Alan. He knocked lightly, then turned the knob, stepping inside. He wasn't wearing a coat, just jeans and a flannel shirt that he hadn't tucked in.

"I heard the door in the dining room open and close," he said by way of explanation for his presence. "Is everything all right?"

"I couldn't sleep. I hope you don't mind me wandering."

Approaching her now, he smiled. "The pool house is for guests." He motioned toward the hot tub on the other side of the pool. "If you want to get in the tub for a soak, it's an experience with the snow falling. There are extra suits in that small chest over there. I'm sure one of Christina's would fit you."

If Lisa was in a bathing suit, Alan would see her tattoos. In a bathing suit, she'd feel practically naked. Being naked—even semi-naked—around him would only be asking for trouble. "I think I'll skip the hot tub tonight."

"It might relax you so you can sleep."

"I'm relaxed. I'm sure when I go back to my room I'll fall asleep."

He lowered himself beside her on the love seat. "You don't look relaxed. Your spine is as straight as a rod. You look like you're ready to bolt."

"You're imagining things. I was cold. I'm getting warm now." She willed herself to loosen up.

"I don't understand you, Lisa. One moment you seem adventurous and free, the next you're guarded and withdrawn. What's up with that?"

"Are you the same all the time—with everybody you meet, with everyone you spend time with?"

"I thought I was until I met you. Around you, in some ways I feel like a teenager again." His hair fell rakishly over his brow. With his flannel shirt open at the neck, the flaps hanging out over his jeans, he looked younger.

"Do you think I make you feel younger?" She was searching for a reason for his attraction to her.

"When I'm around you, I feel an excitement about life I haven't felt in a long time, a sort of buzzing in my blood."

She knew about the buzzing because she was experiencing it, too. "Certainly you've felt that way about other women since your divorce."

"Actually, no, I haven't. I've wanted to. I think I might have even pretended I did. I might have convinced myself that I felt sparks when there weren't any there."

"Why did you do that?"

He shoved his hand through his hair and frowned. "It's complicated."

"Tell me," she suggested, wanting to hear what he had to say.

"You don't want the long, drawn-out history of my love life."

"I want to know if any of what we're feeling is real." After all, maybe kissing her had been a rush. Maybe now he didn't really feel anything except an inkling of sexual interest he might feel with any woman. If that was the case, she'd push him away fast and run hard.

He shifted a bit, his knee brushing hers. He didn't

move it away. Maybe he saw that she needed some real honesty from him, some real sincerity, so she could figure out what she wanted to do next.

"It's an old story, really," he began. "I was in college at the University of Oregon. I wanted to know what kind of world was out there, outside the boundaries of Texas and the Lazy B. I went to Oregon because I could find things I'd never experienced in Texas—the rock climbing, the boating, the ocean not that far away. When I went to college, I was thinking about escaping my roots. Neal had already graduated and was taking over the reins of the ranch from my dad. Before I returned to manage it with him, I wanted to taste life somewhere else."

"That's normal for any kid trying to find his wings," she commented.

"I suppose so. I dated, but nothing serious. Then Christmas of my junior year, I met Sherri at a family party when I came home for the holidays. It sounds terrible to say it, but I was bored and didn't really want to be back home. She'd moved to Rocky Ridge from Oklahoma, and taken a job with her uncle at the home improvement store. She was trying to escape her roots, too, I guess. We dated over the holidays and one night, things went too far. She told me she was on the pill and I believed her."

"She wasn't?"

"She was, but I don't know if she remembered to take it regularly. She didn't tell me that. When I came home at Easter, I found out she was pregnant. There was never any question in my mind what I had to do. I asked her to marry me so we could raise our child together, but we never had real feelings for each other."

He looked straight ahead as if he were looking back and seeing what had gone wrong. "We tried to make it work for ten long years. It just didn't. When Christina was in fifth grade, her grades began falling and the teacher questioned whether there were problems at home. We'd thought we'd covered them really well, but kids...they just soak in everything. And Christina could feel that her mom and I didn't love each other. I was away on business more and more, so I didn't have to be home. Sherri was constantly complaining when I *was* at home. So we let go of the marriage and concentrated on our daughter."

Once again Lisa's heart thumped unbearably hard. Alan had dropped out of college to make a life and accept responsibility. She had left responsibility behind to go to college. In so many ways, they were opposites.

So why was she breathless every time she looked into his eyes? "And you really haven't been involved with anyone since your divorce?"

"Not seriously."

Maybe that meant he couldn't commit. Maybe he was still trying to escape his roots. Maybe seeing what was beyond the Lazy B was still more important than settling down in one place to be with someone he loved.

When Alan moved a little closer, when he slipped his arm around her shoulders, she kept perfectly still. They'd shared one kiss. What were the chances a second one would be just as potent? And if it wasn't, wouldn't that prove there was nothing special here?

"I feel so alive when I'm with you," he murmured, a breath before his lips captured hers.

It didn't even take a second until she was tipsy from the intoxicating rush of desire that went straight to her head, and her heart, her soul and her body. When his tongue coaxed her lips apart and began an erotic invasion, there was no doubt that this chemistry she had with Alan *was* special. He took the kiss deeper and his hands slipped to her breast. He groaned when he realized she wasn't wearing a bra. Their passion escalated so fast, she hardly realized she was unbuttoning his shirt, touching his skin, sifting her fingers through his chest hair. All of it felt so good that she just wanted it to go on and on. She wanted Alan to touch her everywhere and make love to her and—

Make love.

Love didn't happen in an instant. It didn't happen because two people had chemistry and couldn't keep their hands off each other. She thought of Thad and the lines he'd fed her, the things he'd told her, the feelings she'd thought were mutual.

Mutual.

Did she even want anything mutual? Didn't she have a life to find? Hadn't she given up Timothy so that he could have the best of everything?

That meant the best of *her,* too. She wouldn't move away from him. She wouldn't find a life outside of him. She was his backup, his in-case-something-happened-to-

Brian-and-Carrie security. Nothing would ever change that. She had no right kissing Alan like this, endangering everything she was trying to build.

She pulled away from him, gasping from the loss, knowing she was doing what was right, yet wanting him so keenly, she was confused about everything.

To her surprise, he wasn't angry, he just looked perplexed. "This isn't what you want?"

In essence, he was asking, *Am I not what you want?* He was *everything* she wanted, possibly, but not right now. Maybe not ever.

Sitting up, she didn't answer him, just reached for her jacket. "I'm sorry, Alan, I really am, but I can't—"

She couldn't get out any more words or she'd cry. She wouldn't cry in front of him. She didn't want to cry in front of anyone.

She left Alan in the pool house. When she looked back over her shoulder, he was sitting on the love seat, staring into the fire.

Tears came then, whether she wanted them to or not. She swiped them away as she hurried back to her room.

Chapter Seven

Whenever Alan looked at Lisa, she glanced away. He had a terrifically difficult time keeping his attention on the breakfast conversation Friday morning. After another glance at her, during which their gazes met for an interminable moment, he focused on what his daughter was saying to Brian.

"It absolutely purrs. I can give you a ride later if you'd like," she added. "You, too, Uncle Neal. Maude can sit in the back seat because she's got short legs. She'll fit."

Christina had today free from school because the teachers had in-service meetings. He knew in her excitement over her car she was oblivious to how quiet everyone was this morning, including his ex-wife, who'd joined them.

Neal nudged Sherri. "Since Christina is staying, I'll give you a ride home when you're ready."

Christina explained to Lisa, who was sitting beside her, "I'm staying overnight so I can see Dad off tomorrow morning. I know you and Dad and Mr. Summers have a meeting at one with a client. I can occupy myself in the barn. I always find something to do here."

"As opposed to not being able to find things to do at home?" Sherri asked, looking a bit hurt.

"Oh, Mom. You know what I mean."

Although Sherri had been practically monosyllabic this morning—Alan didn't know what *her* problem was—he did know what was bothering Lisa. He should never have kissed her again. He should never have let the kiss get out of hand. Apparently she was too young to even think about a serious relationship yet she'd made it clear an affair wasn't what she was looking for, either. Was she going to isolate herself from men until she was successful? That didn't make much sense. There was more going on beneath the surface with Lisa than he knew about. He was sure of it.

Or else maybe she lacked the maturity to handle a relationship and a commitment.

What was he thinking about? A commitment? He'd just met her!

But you've never felt like this before, an inner voice whispered.

Every once in a while, Brian shot a glance his way, too, with a message that told Alan his friend was watching out for Lisa in a protective way. Why did she need to be protected? Simply because she was young? Or for some other reason? Red flags were going up all over the place, but Alan couldn't decipher what they meant.

After finishing the last of her pancakes, Christina wiped her mouth with her napkin. "Do you want to go out to the barn with me?" she asked Lisa. "We could go for a ride. You don't need her right now, do you, Dad? Mr. Summers?"

Alan let Brian answer.

"She's free until our meeting at one."

"I'd love to go riding again," Lisa replied, as if the thought provided some relief from hanging out at the house with Alan and Brian.

"Give her Blue or Buttercup," Alan warned his daughter.

"I know, Dad. I wouldn't do something stupid like giving her Stormy." Then Christina was on her feet, hugging her mother, telling her she'd see her the next day.

Saying "I'll be back in a little while," Lisa grabbed her coat from a peg on the wall and followed Christina out the door. Soon Neal left, too, and Brian went to his room to take care of e-mails on his laptop.

Maude was quietly clearing the table when Sherri frowned. "So was the car Christina's idea or that secretary's?"

The question surprised Alan. "Christina knew exactly what she wanted. When she makes a decision, she doesn't let anyone sway her, you know that."

"I know I don't want the wrong people influencing her."

"Define 'wrong people.'" Alan was trying to keep from getting irritated.

"People who don't really know her, who don't have her best interests at heart. That secretary is only making nice with Christina to get on your good side. Men are *so* blind."

Instead of rising to the bait, Alan stood. "The fact that Christina and Lisa hit it off, that they talk the same music, like the same clothes and seem to have much in common, shouldn't upset you."

"If they have *anything* in common, it's because of their age, which is considerably younger than *yours*."

"I'm well aware of how old I am. I'm also aware that Christina is still a minor, while Lisa is over the age of consent."

Now Sherri stood, too. "So something *is* going on with you two."

Whatever the chemistry between him and Lisa, he wasn't about to discuss it with his ex-wife. "Lisa is assisting me and Brian on this deal."

"And when you go back to Portland, you're going to have nothing else to do with her?"

"I told you before, this isn't any of your business."

"If she's going to be around Christina at all, it is."

"I doubt if she'll be around Christina after tomorrow. You know, don't you, that once Christina goes off to college, we'll be lucky if she comes back to visit us?"

Suddenly Sherri's eyes became bright with emotion. "I hate the thought of her going so far away. I still don't agree with her majoring in animal sciences. She should be going into premed. The only consolation is that when she's finished with her schooling, she might come back here to work."

He'd wondered why Sherri had accepted so easily the fact that Christina wasn't going to be a doctor. Now he realized she'd had an ulterior motive. She *always* had an ulterior motive. Truthfully, he'd never been sure if she hadn't planned to get pregnant, marry him and inherit the Barretts' way of living.

"I'm dating, too, you know," she said as if some kind of competition was going on.

He could state he wasn't dating Lisa...and he wasn't. The way things were going, they'd be lucky to have a civil working relationship. But Alan believed silence was the best policy with Sherri.

She added, "He's a stockbroker."

Christina had mentioned her mother was dating a stockbroker, but she hadn't told him much else. Alan wouldn't pump her for information. "How did you meet?" he asked, because Sherri hadn't dated much since their divorce.

"I met him at one of those career fairs the high school held."

"What does Christina think of him?" He wanted Sherri's take on it.

"She likes Russ. She thinks he's a little stiff, but he isn't really. He's just very polite with her."

That was good, Alan supposed. "Is it serious?"

Sherri gave a little shrug. "I don't know yet. We've

only been dating a couple of months and I certainly don't want to rush into anything. Neither should you."

"I'm glad you're letting me know what's going on in your life, but I don't have any more say in yours than you have in mine. If I don't like this Russ, it doesn't mean you'll stop seeing him, does it?"

"No, of course not."

"My point exactly."

"She's too young for you, Alan."

He'd had enough of this. "I've dated women since our divorce and you've never commented. Why now?"

"Because I've seen the way you look at her."

That shook him up. "I think you've been watching too many romantic comedies."

"Turn cynical on me if you must, but I've seen you with women you've dated before. We've gone to the same charity functions and I've spotted your picture in the paper with them. In the past, I got the idea you didn't care who you were with. You just wanted a warm body for some fun. That's what you wanted from me when we met, wasn't it?"

"We were twenty. I thought that's what we *both* wanted."

"If I hadn't gotten pregnant, we wouldn't have lasted."

"No, we wouldn't have."

After a heavy silence, she admitted grudgingly, "You've been a good father."

But not a good husband, he noted to himself, knowing it was true. He'd never regretted having Christina, but he'd resented Sherri for the way it had happened—for either her naivete, or her manipulation of the situation. Still, he had to give her her due. "You've been a good mother."

"Once Christina's on her own, things will change," Sherri said wistfully.

"Maybe. But we'll always have her best interests to think about first, no matter what she makes of her future."

"If one of us hooks up with someone, that will change things, too."

"We'll deal with it, just as we've dealt with everything else."

Without rancor this time, Sherri asked, "Is there ever a time when you aren't confident you can handle your life? You're always so in control of everything. I've always envied that."

"You've resented it, too."

"Yes, I guess I have." She checked her watch. "I'd better be going. I have a lot of errands to run today."

"Have a date tonight?"

She blushed. "Actually, yes I do. I have a hair appointment and a nail appointment..." She trailed off, apparently realizing she was revealing some of the excitement she felt.

Going to the sideboard, she picked up her purse. "I know you don't want to hear it, but try to be a little...prudent with this secretary."

When he finally thought he and Sherri had made some headway in communicating, she'd say something that would annoy him all over again. "I could give you the same advice."

His ex-wife replied, "I'm not trying to recapture my youth."

After that parting shot, she left.

Alan heard the clink of china in the kitchen and realized Maude had discreetly left the dining room when his discussion with Sherri had begun. Now he took a few dishes, stacked them and took them to the counter.

"I didn't hear much," the housekeeper said, rinsing the plates one by one before she plopped them in the dishwasher.

"I suppose you stuffed napkins in your ears?"

"No, I ran the water."

He'd started to turn away and go to his office when she added, "I think Sherri's right about one thing."

Although Maude never meddled needlessly, she gave her opinion when she felt a member of the family needed to hear it. "Just what was she right about?" he asked.

"You look at Lisa differently than you've looked at other women, and there's a connection between the two of you that anyone in the room can feel."

"She's young, Maude."

"I know she's twenty-one, but there's something in her eyes that tells me she's much older than her years."

"I see that, too."

"Don't rush headlong into anything, but I don't think you should cut off your nose to spite your face, either."

"She doesn't want to get involved," he said honestly.

Maude shrugged. "Then I guess you'll either have to walk away or convince her otherwise."

Right now, he knew walking away would be the easiest course for both of them. But was easy the way he wanted to live his life?

Later that afternoon, Lisa was ready to scream. Although she had taken copious notes while she'd walked the for-sale property with Alan, Brian and their clients, the awkwardness she felt with Alan was like a tightrope that she knew was going to break soon. She couldn't ignore him and he couldn't ignore her. But they were doing a darn good job of trying.

Now, as the others left the springhouse they'd examined, she lingered. So did Alan. Only a high window let in the daylight, but in the shadows, she could see he had something on his mind.

The low murmur of men's voices floated through the open door. Lisa heard the caw of a bird, the hum of a small plane overhead, but the noises couldn't distract her from Alan. They couldn't keep her from looking into his blue eyes.

"I want to ask you something." His voice was almost terse.

"What?"

"When we return to Portland, faxes and phone calls and meetings about this deal will go on for a long time. Do you want to be a part of it? Or do you want me to persuade Brian to have another associate sit in?"

She didn't know if Alan was asking for her benefit or his. "Which would you prefer?"

"This is your decision, Lisa."

After a few moments of silence, she answered, "I don't see why we can't work together professionally. I can't believe how much I've learned from this trip, and I'd like to see this project through to completion. I also don't want to give Brian any reason to think he can't count on me, or you, either, for that matter."

Alan looked as if he was proud of what she'd just said, and that meant a lot to her…maybe too much.

He was suddenly a few steps closer. "I want you to know that if we continue to work together, nothing will happen that shouldn't. I'll make sure we're not in a compromising situation, and nothing I do will give you any reason to think of me as anything but a business associate."

His words made her heart heavy. This was what she wanted, wasn't it? Her focus went to his mouth and how much pleasure he could give her. She remembered touching his chest, feeling his heat, being inflamed by his passion.

Don't think about it, she scolded herself.

His gaze was on her lips…on her face. He couldn't know she melted every time he looked at her. He couldn't know how her heart lifted when he entered the room. He couldn't know that whenever they were together, she was happy to be around him, but hurt because of what they would never have.

"I want you to know how much I enjoyed this trip, Alan. How much I enjoyed meeting your daughter. She's really wonderful. You have so much to be proud of."

"I think you'd become friends if you had more time together."

"I think we would, too. Who knows? If you spend a lot of time in Portland and she comes to visit you there, maybe she and I can go shopping together."

"Women and shopping, the great bonding experience."

Lisa smiled, and yet she was crying inside because this felt so much like goodbye.

It *was* goodbye. She felt as if she'd said so many goodbyes in her life—to her parents, her aunt, to Thad and, most painful of all, to Timothy—that she'd lost a huge part of herself, a huge part of her heart. She didn't want to say goodbye to Alan, but what choice did she have?

"Christina and I are going to watch a movie tonight. She picked up one about a horse that breaks its leg, then goes on to win the Breeders' Cup. You're welcome to join us."

"It's probably better if I don't. I'm still typing up all my notes on my laptop. It will give me a head start when I get to the office on Monday."

Alan nodded, as if he'd known that's what her answer would be. Then he motioned for her to precede him out of the springhouse. As she passed in front of him, she caught the scent of his aftershave and felt his gaze on her back as she walked out into the sunshine.

She wouldn't forget this trip to Texas…not ever.

"Tell Miss Sanders this isn't a good time, Ralph. I'll talk to her tomorrow." Alan's voice came from the intercom in his penthouse Sunday evening, sounding very tired.

Lisa asked Ralph, "May I talk to him myself? I think he's sick and doesn't want anyone to know it. But he might need some help."

Ralph let her take his place at the intercom.

This morning, as they'd flown back from Texas, Alan had looked more than a little under the weather. He'd been absolutely gray. Brian hadn't seemed to notice, in the way men don't notice those things, but *she* had. She and Alan had hardly spoken on the trip home. She was still raw from everything that had happened at the Lazy B, including the decision to put Alan out of her mind in a romantic sense. She cared about him and was afraid he was pulling a macho act and might be really sick.

Last night as she'd stayed awake thinking and feeling, she'd realized that she *couldn't* say goodbye to Alan. He'd already made a place for himself in her heart and she was worried about him.

That's why she was here.

She pressed the intercom button. "Alan, it's me. Do you have someone with you?"

There was a hesitation, then his voice came through the speaker. "No."

"Then you don't have a good reason why I shouldn't come up, do you? I have some forms on the resort that need to be signed." She did—although they didn't need to be signed tonight. But any excuse at this point was a good one.

"All right." He gave in angrily. "Bring them up."

Triumphantly she smiled at Ralph.

Like a coconspirator, he mused, "Mr. Barrett did look tired when he came in. He didn't go out for supper like he usually does."

"I'll make sure everything's all right. If he needs a doctor, I'll call down."

Ralph worried his lower lip with his teeth. "You really have papers for Mr. Barrett?"

Lisa wiggled the envelope. "Right here."

Ralph went behind his desk and pressed the button to open the private elevator to the penthouse.

Lisa didn't feel all that triumphant as the elevator rose and she stepped off onto Alan's floor. What if he wouldn't let her inside? What if he simply snatched the papers from her and that was that?

So be it. She couldn't do more than she could do…or more than he'd let her do.

She'd spent all afternoon debating whether she should come over here tonight or not. But once the decision was made, she wasn't turning back.

At his door, she knocked once, then knocked again.

When he opened it, her resolve intensified. He looked terrible, dressed in wrinkled sweats with his feet bare. His hair was disheveled and he had dark circles under his eyes. He was holding on to the door frame as if his life depended on it.

Still, his eyes were turbulent and annoyed. "Give me the papers. I'll sign them and have them messengered to Brian tomorrow."

"They have to be witnessed," she said sweetly, pushing past him. Everything was as it had been the last time she was here. Not even a magazine out of place.

Appearing downright angry now, he didn't move from the door. "Lisa, what are you doing here?"

She waved the envelope.

Frowning, he shut the door, took a couple of seconds, then made his way to the sofa…very slowly.

"Alan, tell me what's wrong. You look awful."

Lowering himself onto the seat, he dropped his head into his hands and then groaned. "Some kind of damn bug. Leave, Lisa. You don't want to get it."

As close as they'd been at times in Texas, if she was going to get whatever he had, she would. But she had a strong constitution and she doubted it would happen. She suspected Alan had let himself get run-down, hadn't had enough sleep with all the balls he was juggling.

She sank onto the sofa beside him. "We were together in Texas, remember? I've probably already been exposed. So tell me what I can do for you."

He shook his head. "Just leave me alone."

"Do you have a fever?"

"Not that I know of."

"That's because you didn't take your temperature, did you?"

"Go away, Lisa. I'll sleep this off and be as good as new tomorrow."

"With a little help, you might feel better tonight."

He turned toward her, but closed his eyes for a moment

as if the movement made him dizzy. "I don't need someone to take care of me."

"Don't you?" she retorted. "Looks to me as if you do. Have you eaten anything?"

He didn't nod and he didn't answer.

"I thought not. How's your stomach?"

"It's fine…until I move around a lot," he grumbled.

She couldn't help but smile. "Did you ever think the best place for you to be is in bed?"

"What if I told you I was there before you disturbed me?"

"I wouldn't believe you."

He sighed. "You're right. I only go to bed to sleep, and to…" The look he gave her was smoldering in spite of the way he felt, and she saw that his defenses were down. She had to make sure hers weren't.

"Do you have a thermometer?"

He leaned back on the sofa, tilting his head against the cushion. "In the medicine cabinet."

It took her only a minute to find his bedroom and the bathroom beyond. It was luxurious and large. There was a black whirlpool tub and a walk-in shower with a beautiful pressed-glass door. His medicine cabinet was practically empty, though it held a box of bandages, a bottle of peroxide, a vial of acetaminophen and the thermometer. Plucking the items from the shelf, she hurried back to the sofa. The thermometer was one of those that beeped after it recorded the temperature. It had never been used. She tore the paper from it and touched Alan's arm.

His eyes flew open.

"Here, let's see what we've got."

"We've got a man who's being bothered by a woman," he muttered.

She slipped the thermometer into his mouth. Meanwhile, she went into his kitchen to see if he had anything that might make him feel better. She didn't find much—a bag with two bagels that were stale, soda and a lone apple that had seen better days.

The thermometer beeped and Lisa practically ran to fetch it from Alan's mouth. Her stomach dipped when she saw what it said. "It's 101.8. You should call your doctor."

"I don't need a doctor. I just need to sleep this off."

Sitting down beside him, she turned sideways to look at him until her jean-clad leg brushed against his knee. "I'm worried."

With a blown-out breath, he shook his head. "Don't be."

"I'll make a deal with you. I won't call an ambulance if you promise to call your doctor if it hits 102."

One corner of his lips quirked up. "That's a deal? That's blackmail."

"No, that's just my way of dealing with a stubborn man who doesn't know what to do for his own good."

Alan wrapped his arms around himself as if he was cold. With that temperature he probably had chills. "The first thing we've got to do is get some liquids into you. I'd prefer something hot, but you don't have any tea."

"I hate tea."

"Too bad. I'm going to get you settled and then go buy

some supplies. I'll be gone fifteen minutes, tops. There's a convenience store at the corner. I'll be right back."

Alan closed his eyes again and didn't even seem to notice she stood up.

Minutes later she'd gathered what she needed to deal with a man who was too tall and heavy to move, and too stubborn to do what she wanted. She snapped a pillow onto the opposite end of the couch.

"Lie back," she ordered.

He opened his eyes and stared at the pillow.

"If you won't go to bed, the bed will come to you. Lie down," she repeated.

His smile was crooked. "So you can have your way with me?"

"Don't you wish."

As soon as he'd stretched out, she took the pair of socks she'd found in his drawer and slipped them onto his feet. "The last thing you need is to get more chilled."

Lifting a blanket she'd found in a closet, she threw it over him. A few minutes later, she'd set half of a toasted bagel and a glass of clear soda with ice on the coffee table beside him. "Sip that if you can. Try to eat the bagel before you take the acetaminophen. Hopefully, we can break that fever."

After he did as she suggested, he settled himself deeper into the pillow. "The room moves less if I keep still."

"Then keep still."

As she stood again, he clasped her wrist. "Don't go."

"I was just going to run to the store."

His gaze met hers. "I don't know why I said that. Of course you're going to go. Just leave, Lisa. Really. I'll be fine."

Taking one of the large pillows from the stack of four, she dragged it over to the sofa and set it near the arm where he lay. Then she sank down onto the floor. "Try to get some rest. I'll go to the store in the morning. I'm not going anywhere now."

He must have seen the determination on her face and heard it in her voice. Instead of arguing, he settled himself again on the pillow and closed his eyes.

She listened to the sound of Alan's breathing, feeling as if this was exactly where she belonged.

Chapter Eight

"Don't jump the fence, Christina. It's too high! He'll throw you."

Lisa came awake and quickly vaulted out of the oversize recliner.

Alan had thrown off his cover and was tossing and turning on the sofa.

. Beside him now, on her knees, she threw her arm across his chest. "Alan, it's all right. It's just a dream."

His T-shirt was soaked with perspiration, but he still seemed hot and clammy.

"Alan," she said again, trying to break through his dream.

When his eyes flew open, he stared at her for a few seconds, then stilled. "Christina tried to jump a fence with her horse when she was eight. She broke her arm. Being a witness to it was one of the worst moments of my life."

Lisa wanted to say she understood. She wanted to tell him that when she saw Timothy headed for a fall, all she wanted to do was run and scoop him up and keep him safe. Yet if she told Alan that, she'd have to tell him the rest, and this simply wasn't the time. He was shivering and his complexion still lacked color.

"Christina's going to be all right when she goes to college. You'll see. She'll make you proud."

"Sometimes she's still too headstrong…too naive."

"Age will take care of that. Alan, you really ought to be in bed. You need to change clothes and get warm and dry."

After a few moments of silence, he asked, "What time is it?"

"Around eleven. It's time for more medicine. More liquids."

He hiked himself up and closed his eyes.

"Still dizzy?"

"Only when I move."

"Are you going to let me help you to your room?"

His gaze was long and assessing as he stared at her. "Why are you doing this? Staying here with me."

"Because you need help."

"You'd do this for anyone who needed help?"

"I'd like to think I would."

"Brian would have a fit if he knew you were here," he muttered.

"Are you worried about *your* partnership with him?"

"No, but I'm worried about your relationship with him, whatever that is."

"I told you—"

"Yeah, I know what you told me." He swung his legs to the floor. "Carrie and Brian befriended you when you moved to Portland. Just how did you meet them, anyway?"

If she didn't share some of her story, they couldn't get closer. She *did* want to get close to this man. Maybe if she gave him a little bit at a time, he could come to accept who she was. He could integrate it with who she intended to be.

"I ran away from my aunt in Seattle, found a room here and a job waitressing. One day I got sick and ended up in the E.R. That led me to Carrie."

"She volunteers at Portland General, doesn't she?"

"Yes, she does. We met and connected, and that's how we became friends." That was the shortened version of her story, but Alan seemed to accept it.

Rising to her feet before he could ask any more questions, she said, "Let me help you to your room."

He swore and grumbled, "I hate this."

As he came to his feet, she slipped her arm around his waist. "Nobody likes being sick."

"I have to make a pit stop in the bathroom. And I *don't* need help with that!"

She grinned. "Are you sure? If you end up in a heap on the floor, I'll have to call Ralph."

"Heaven forbid," he muttered. "Believe me. I'll be fine."

A few moments later she left him standing in the bathroom doorway. "Where are your pajamas?"

"I don't wear pajamas."

After she absorbed that, she announced, "I'll go to the kitchen and get you more soda and medicine. If you're under the covers when I come back in, not wearing pajamas won't matter."

She thought she heard him swear again when she left the room, but she wasn't sure. She was worried about him, but knew his pride was important to him. If he couldn't manage, she *could* always call Ralph…or Brian.

No, Brian *wouldn't* like her being here like this. Would he understand? She hoped so. It was simply something she had to do.

To pay Alan back for his kindness in Texas?

Yes. She was simply being a Good Samaritan but she was also acting on her growing feelings for Alan. She couldn't deny them any longer.

She took her time in the kitchen, refilling Alan's glass with fresh ice and soda, toasting another half bagel, shaking out two more pills. When she returned to the bedroom, he had the covers pulled up to his chin and looked as if he was shivering again.

Walking into his bathroom, she went to the long narrow cupboard that lined the wall next to the shower. Now she opened it and groped around a little, finding what she was looking for—a heat pack she could warm in the microwave. As athletic as Alan was, she figured he might have one on hand.

A short time later, she'd wrapped the heat pack in a towel and tucked it in by his side. After she took his temperature—it was 101 now—she asked, "Is there anything else you need?"

"I'll be fine. Go on home."

"You're beginning to sound like a broken record. I'm not going anywhere until I'm sure you're on the mend."

"You need your rest, too."

"I know. I'm going to stretch out on the sofa. I'll come in and check on you in a little while."

He closed his eyes. "How am I going to repay you for this?"

"That's just it, Alan. You don't have to." She watched him for a while longer, and seeing that he was dozing off, she went back to the living room, her heart feeling warm and even a little light...because he needed her.

The living room was as black as midnight when Lisa awakened. For a moment she wondered where she was, and then she remembered—Alan's penthouse. A night-light glowed in the hallway. She went down the corridor toward it and stepped into his bedroom. He was turned on his side, facing the windows, sound asleep.

Should she wake him to give him more medication? Probably not. He needed rest. But what if he awakened and needed her, and she fell sound asleep again?

The king-size bed was huge, and Alan was under the covers on one side. The spread was undisturbed on the other. Sleepy herself, she stretched out on top of the covers and listened to him breathe. If she stayed here, she'd feel him move if he became restless, if he had another bad dream, if he needed anything. She'd be right here.

Yawning widely, she assured herself sleeping beside Alan was the only practical thing to do. Besides being practical, she just wanted to be near him. It was easier to admit that truth to herself now.

When Lisa woke the following morning, everything registered at once. She was still on top of the covers, but she was rolled close to Alan, her arm across his chest. His hand was on the back of her head, as if he'd been running his fingers through her hair. They were cuddled together as if they'd...as if they'd—

As she tried to disentangle herself, he stirred and opened his eyes. "Don't panic," he told her, as if he'd known she was about to. "You're still on top of the covers and completely clothed."

She certainly was, thank goodness. But then she saw the edge of her tattoo peeking out from under the sleeve of her sweater.

She quickly jerked her arm from his chest, scooted over a few inches and sat up against the headboard. "I don't know what happened. I came in to check on you and just decided to lie here in case you needed anything. I must have fallen sound asleep."

"And the moon did the rest?" he teased. "The pull of gravity and all?"

"You're feeling better," she said almost accusingly.

He laughed. "I certainly hope so. Yesterday isn't a

day I'd want to repeat. Well, at least most parts of it." He hiked himself up against the headboard as well, and the sheet dropped down to his navel.

Lisa swallowed hard, knowing she should get out of the bed…Alan's bed. She couldn't seem to make herself move.

"The dizziness is gone?" she asked.

"I won't know for sure until I stand up, but it's probably not a good idea, since I'm naked under here."

She felt like an idiot, in way over her head. Maybe that was because she and Thad had always fumbled in the dark, never really seeing each other naked. They'd never discussed being naked, or making love and what should come after.

Making love.

That got her out of Alan's bed. She scooted to the edge and was on her feet, knowing she was blushing. "You should probably take it easy today. I'll run down to that convenience store and get you some groceries."

He leaned forward and the sheet fell *below* his navel. Her gaze dropped and she couldn't look away.

"Lisa, you don't have to buy me groceries. I'll get something later."

With effort, she focused on his face. "You might be dizzy when you get out of bed. It'll take me ten minutes, tops. I'll be right back, then I'll go away and let you alone. I have to go home and do laundry, finish unpacking—"

Before she could compute what was happening, Alan had pulled the spread from the bed and stood with it wrapped around his waist. "Thank you for staying last night."

Her heart was doing that double-time beat again and she could hardly catch her breath. "You're welcome."

"I know you're probably not going to believe this, but I can't remember the last time somebody cared enough to go out of their way for me."

"You probably haven't been sick very much."

"No, I haven't, but your staying here last night meant a lot. So don't try to brush it off as if it didn't matter."

"I'm sorry about…the way we woke up."

He grinned, looking absolutely rakish with morning stubble, tousled hair and the spread wrapped around him like a toga. "Apparently I was enjoying having you in my arms. But we both know all the reasons why letting that happen again wouldn't be a good idea."

Yes, they did know all the reasons. "We have to be practical," she agreed. Ungluing her gaze from his chest, she hurried on. "And speaking of being practical, do you want toast or English muffins?"

Seeing he wouldn't deter her from her mission to feed him, he replied, "Toast will be fine."

Then before he either let the spread drop or walked across the room to her, she rushed out to the living room. Nothing had happened between them last night…absolutely nothing. He hadn't even kissed her again!

Yet she still remembered the brush of his chest hair under her fingertips. She was falling for Alan Barrett whether she wanted to or not.

* * *

Lisa held Timothy as he pointed to one of the mountain goats at the Portland Zoo Tuesday afternoon and his mouth rounded in an O. He delighted in everything here and she tried to remember each expression on his face, each giggle, each sound because he'd discovered something new and exciting for a three-year-old.

As she glanced over her shoulder, she caught sight of Carrie, who'd obviously been watching her. There was a little furrow on her brow, and Lisa suspected what that furrow was about. Did Carrie wonder if she was doing the right thing, letting Lisa into Timothy's life? Did she ask herself every day if Lisa might eventually want her child back?

Lisa could never do that to this woman who had given her so much. Not only a home and a family, but trust and love and hope. She would never do that to Timothy, because he deserved to always be secure. He deserved to always know who his mom and dad were. Carrie and Brian *were* his mom and dad. Lisa had given him birth, but Carrie was his mom.

Reinforcing that conclusion, Timothy wiggled in Lisa's arms, wanting down. He ran to Carrie. "Mommy, Mommy! Look, look at the goats."

Carrie hunkered down with him. "I see the goats. Maybe we should count them."

Lisa felt as if she were playing hooky today, even though she wasn't. Because she'd gone to Texas and given up part of her weekend, Brian had insisted she take a day off this week. After studying his schedule and seeing which day was the lightest, she'd chosen today. She'd been so tempted yesterday to call Alan to see how he was feeling, yet she knew she shouldn't. She also knew she was scared. She was falling for him big time and leaving herself wide open to rejection and abandonment, all over again. His life was full of work and his daughter, and maybe even his ex-wife, for all Lisa knew. Sherri was a beautiful woman, in his league, his age. The age difference seemed to be a huge impediment to him. It wasn't to Lisa. Not anymore. In fact, she'd figured out she was attracted to his maturity, his experience, his view of life.

After the mountain goats, Carrie pushed Timothy's stroller as they visited the bears and then the monkeys. For February, the day was beautiful—unusually bright, though clouds often skittered across the sun. They'd stopped to watch the elephants when suddenly they had company.

Brian grinned broadly as he kissed Carrie and then stopped to talk to his son in his stroller. "We thought we'd join you. What do you think? Are you going to show your dad what you like best about the zoo?"

While Brian was talking to Timothy, Carrie turned to Alan who had stopped a few feet away. "Hi, Alan. This is a surprise."

Though Alan addressed Carrie, his gaze was on Lisa, on her red jacket, on her jeans, on her face. He tipped his Stetson back with his forefinger. "We were in a meeting that finished early not too far from here. Brian mentioned you and Lisa were taking Timothy to the zoo today. I had something I wanted to discuss with Lisa, so I tagged along. Actually, I'm hoping she's had enough of the zoo by now. Have you?"

She didn't know what they had to discuss. Business? Or something personal? A bit warily, she asked, "What did you have in mind?"

"Since the sky's almost blue and the weather's cooperating, I thought we could take a drive up to Bridal Veil Falls State Park."

Brian glanced over at Alan, looking worried, but Carrie said, "That sounds like a lovely idea."

Bridal Veil Falls were magnificent. Carrie had told Lisa that's where Brian had proposed to her. Lisa's heart thudded hard as she wondered why Alan wanted to drive her there.

Moving a little closer to him, she asked, "Is this a date?"

"Close to it. Do you want to come?"

Oh, she *wanted* to come. But should she?

Stop being a coward, she told herself. *At least risk finding out how interested he is in you.*

Fifteen minutes later, Lisa was seated in Alan's Jaguar as they headed toward the park. They'd been silent thus far and now she commented, "If you want to talk, we don't have to go to Bridal Veil Falls to do that. We can go to my apartment or your condo."

She felt his shift of attention for a few moments. "Do you think that's wise? I thought someplace neutral where we can't get caught up in body heat might be a good idea. Besides, I haven't been here since college."

"The falls are magnificent," she agreed with a little sigh. She had a feeling that today all of her attention would be on Alan, not on the falls.

After he parked, they took the upper trail that led to the viewing platform. A wooden railing on either side of the walkway protected visitors as they strolled to the overlook. Lisa and Alan were the only sightseers here right now.

There was an awesome feeling about the place—the high rock cliffs; the white-capped green-blue river below, the double-decker falls, which indeed did look like a bridal veil, especially when the wind blew the misty water. Each step Lisa and Alan took seemed to bring them into contact, either with elbows, hips or glances. They didn't talk as they walked the path, and she was glad about that. Talking would only break the mood and the beauty. She didn't know what he was going to say to her. This might be his attempt to let her down easy. Bring her to a beautiful setting and tell her they were absolutely wrong for each other. After all, they were, weren't they?

Finally standing on the viewing platform, she was glad for the few rays of sun that managed to seep through the clouds and spray light over the water and rocks.

Alan stood next to her as they gazed at the falls, letting the natural noises of nature surround them—the splash of water, the rush of wind, the call of gulls.

"I used to come up here to put things in perspective," he said, finally breaking the silence.

"Problems seem smaller up here?" she asked.

"*I* seem smaller up here. While I'm working and living and planning, I think my life is all there is. My concerns fill up my world and I forget there are places where silence and calm can solve problems…where making a deal doesn't matter…where there's something bigger than I can ever hope to be."

"Are you a man of faith?" she asked.

"I went to church weekly until I went to college. What I learned stuck. Now I just concentrate on trying to do the right thing whether it's in business or my personal life. What about you?"

"I went to church with my parents until they died. Aunt Edna couldn't get out much and my world had fallen apart then. Going to church just didn't seem to have the power to solve my problems."

"What problems were those?"

His blue eyes were so serious and she knew he wanted something deeper from her than what she'd been giving him. But if she gave him that, she was afraid she'd lose the connection that had developed, and suddenly it meant so much. She respected Alan in a way she'd never respected a man before.

And suddenly, with all her heart, she knew she didn't just respect him. She was in love with him!

The revelation filled her with joy and happiness…but also fear.

Trying to force all of the emotion into a box she could open later, she confided in Alan.

"I felt as if I didn't have a place anywhere, as if there was no one I could turn to. That's why after I graduated, I came back to Portland on my own."

"That was gutsy."

"Don't think I'm brave, Alan. If I was, I would have—" Her voice caught. She had prayed and prayed and prayed about what to do about the baby and what was best for the child she carried. When Brian and Carrie had come into her life, they'd been a sign…at least that's what she'd thought. True bravery would have been to keep her child.

Alan's arms went around Lisa then, protecting her from the wind, protecting her from her tears, from self-doubts that seem to be growing larger each day rather than smaller.

"I think you're much more mature than any twenty-one year old I've ever met. But in spite of that maturity, in spite of your conquer-the-world attitude, I sense a vulnerability underneath. I don't want to hurt you, Lisa."

"I don't want to hurt *you*," she managed to whisper.

"I've taken a lot more hard knocks than you have, I'm sure. I'm used to them. But that's why I'm worried about what I'm feeling for you."

"It's not just chemistry," she stated.

"Isn't it? Damn it, Lisa, you're beautiful, young and energetic and vibrant. What man wouldn't be attracted to you?"

"There's a whole bunch," she assured him with a smile. Then seriously, she added, "This goes way beyond chemistry between us. I mean, I'll admit, you turn me on big time."

His cheeks darkened even with the cool wind blowing around them.

"I know some people would say I'm looking for a father figure, since I lost my dad," she murmured. "But if I want a father figure, Brian's it. You're different. I feel on top of the world with you. I feel as if we could talk day and night for months and never run out of things to say."

As he took her face between his hands, she knew they both felt more than chemistry. His lips were hot and demanding as they covered hers. His large palm slid to the back of her head as he plunged his tongue into her mouth, and she kissed him back in a way she'd never kissed a man before. She wanted to crawl inside of him. She wanted to be joined with him. She wanted to make love with him and have him teach her everything she didn't know. When she thought about Alan's hands touching her, his lips caressing other parts of her body, his fingers stroking her skin, she became even dizzier, more excited, more thrilled.

Standing in this awesome place, she held on to this man she'd fallen in love with. If only she could convince him age didn't matter. If only she could convince him that she was a different person now than she used to be.

He didn't know the person she used to be. That was both wonderful and dreadful—wonderful because he wasn't judging her for her past, but dreadful because when he found out about it, he would.

On that thought, she slid her hand from his shoulder to the back of his neck under his hat. She wanted this kiss to go on forever and ever and ever.

But as all things in this life, it couldn't. She was still holding on, responding with all the desire welling up inside of her, when Alan slowed everything down. His hands clasped her upper arms and he reluctantly pulled away. As they stood gazing into each other's eyes, he suddenly let go, turned away from her and swiped off his Stetson. He let the wind blow about him, tousling his hair, lifting the lapel of his jacket.

What was he thinking? There was only one way to find out. "Alan?"

Swiveling to face her again, he ran his thumb over the rim of his hat, then plunked it back on his head. "All right," he said, as if he'd come to some conclusion.

"All right?" She didn't know what that meant. He'd obviously been fighting an inner battle and one side or the other had won.

"How would you like to go out with me tomorrow night? It's Valentine's Day."

She wanted to jump up and down, twirl in a circle and sing "Alleluia." How mature would that be? Instead, she just grinned at him. "I'd love to. What do you have in mind?"

"We need to get to know each other better. We need to figure out if we both really want this. So what if I pick you up about seven? We'll have a quiet dinner and see where we can go from there."

"Dinner, where?" She added quickly, "I need to know how to dress."

"I joined a private club in the fall. There are small dining rooms for special occasions. I'll see if I can reserve one of those. They require a suit, so you can judge what you should wear from that."

She could go all-out. She could keep it very simple. Maybe she'd ask Jillian for her opinion. She could ask Carrie, but—

"Are you going to tell Brian we're going out?" she asked him.

"I'm not going to keep it from him, but I'm not going to shout it from the rooftops, either."

"I don't want to affect your friendship or your business relationship with him."

"You won't. We're going to dinner, Lisa. There's nothing wrong with that."

Yes, they were going to dinner, and Alan might or might not tell Brian. They were going to a private club where she guessed very few people would see them. Were Alan's plans for Valentine's Day special and intimate? Or had he chosen an evening like this so they wouldn't be seen in public together, so he wouldn't *have* to make explanations to friends or colleagues?

The age difference between them wasn't going to go away, but neither were her feelings for Alan. Maybe after tomorrow night, she would know whether she should jump in with two feet or not.

Yet she had the feeling her heart already knew the answer to that, and any precautions she might try to take against heartache would already be too late.

Chapter Nine

"Oh, my gosh!" Lisa exclaimed when Alan escorted her out of her building and she saw the shiny white stretch limo at the curb. She'd thought she was prepared for tonight. She'd decided she was going to enjoy being Cinderella for the evening and face reality in the morning. Didn't she deserve one night of fantasy? Didn't any woman?

A chauffeur was standing by the back door of the limo and he opened it.

"You went all-out," she said to Alan, who looked too sexy for words in his Western-cut suit jacket, black bolo tie and black Stetson.

"It's Valentine's Day."

When she'd opened her door to him, his gaze had traveled down her red knit dress, come to rest on the silver concho belt that she'd slung around her hips and returned to her face with a hunger that both terrified her and thrilled her. He was still looking at her that way.

Could she satisfy that hunger? Would she be a disappointment to him? "I suppose I could have brought my car," he told her, "but that wouldn't have been nearly as much fun. Come on, climb in and see what's inside."

As she slid onto the leather seat, Alan joined her. He pointed to the magnum of champagne on the seat across from them. Beside it sat a silver warming dish. "I thought we'd have a glass of Dom Perignon and an appetizer on the way to dinner. What do you think?"

"Can I peek?" Excitement bubbled inside of her because he *was* making her feel like Cinderella.

He grinned. "Sure, you can peek."

If she just sat there next to him wanting to kiss him, wanting him to kiss her, she'd start shaking. So she opened the top of the warmer and saw stuffed mushrooms inside. "Do we have napkins?"

He laughed, deeply and richly. It was a sound that said he appreciated her. She so hoped that was true. All day she'd mulled over why he was taking her to a private club. Because he didn't want them to be seen together in public? Or simply because the night would be more intimate? If the opportunity arose, she'd ask him. Until then, she was simply going to enjoy everything he'd planned.

"Oh, I have napkins all right. Do you want to take off your shawl until we get where we're going?"

She eyed him. "Are you going to take off your hat?"

"A Texan only takes off his hat when he goes to bed, and then it's not that far away. Don't you like hats?"

He was definitely amused by her question, and she found she liked lightening his mood and making him smile. Still, she answered him seriously. "It shadows your face. I can't tell at all what you're thinking or feeling."

In a swift motion, he tossed his hat onto the seat next to the champagne magnum. "What do you see?" he asked huskily.

His blue eyes were mysterious with thoughts and feelings she couldn't read. Yet she guessed what they were. "I see a man who wants to enjoy tonight as much as I do."

"You're a good reader of eyes," he teased. Then his hands went to her shawl and slid it from her shoulders.

She could feel his fingers drag across her back. She could smell the pine scent of his aftershave. She could sense the heat they were both generating, and the evening had just begun.

Lifting her chin, he ran his thumb from side to side over it. "I'd kiss you, but I don't want to mess up your lipstick before we even get started." Then he took the bottle of champagne from the ice and expertly opened it.

Soon he had the golden liquid poured into crystal flutes for each of them. When he handed her hers, she took it. "Can I ask you something?" she murmured.

"You can ask me anything. Well…almost anything," he joked.

"Did you have trouble concentrating today? Or was it just another day in the month?" In spite of herself, she was totally invested in what happened tonight and needed to know he was, too.

"I couldn't work longer than fifteen minutes on anything specific," he admitted wryly. "Is that what you mean?"

"Because you were looking forward to tonight…or because you had doubts?"

After a few moments of silence, he ran his hand through his hair. "Oh, I still have doubts, and I think you do, too. But tonight is about getting to know each other better and I looked forward to that all day."

She honestly got the feeling that Alan meant exactly what he said. That he was a bit on edge because *he* didn't know what was going to happen next, yet was looking forward to whatever did.

She took a sip of the champagne, then wrinkled her nose. "It tickles."

"You've never had champagne before?"

"No. If you haven't guessed, I didn't come from a background of champagne and stuffed mushrooms. My mom was a dental hygienist, my dad an electrician. We lived in a Cape Cod house in an old neighborhood and my room had slanted ceilings. It was yellow and I loved it. My mom made the curtains herself. That sort of gives you a picture of how I grew up."

He nodded. "Quite different from me learning about the price of beef before I went to school, and how to cut cows from a herd. Although my parents lacked for nothing, they made sure Neal and I knew the value of a hard day's work. We never took our life for granted."

Alan's upbringing showed. The man he'd become told her that those early values had lasted. "I think I *did* take my life for granted," she confided. "I mean I lived in this bubble and thought everything would always be perfect—that my parents would always be around. I'd go to my prom, graduate, become something they'd be proud of, then I'd have a family and they'd dote on my kids."

Her throat closed and she stopped when she realized what she'd said. Clearing her throat, she recovered quickly. "I don't take anything for granted anymore. When your world changes drastically, quickly, nothing's ever the same again. It's like something happens in an instant, and you have to spend years trying to make everything right again."

"What did you have to make right again?" he asked gently.

"I had to stop feeling like a victim. I had to take control, run my own life and grow up fast."

They were sitting terrifically close, his thigh lodged against hers. Extending his arm around her shoulders, he leaned even nearer and kissed her temple. "Getting to know you better was a very good idea."

Her heart told her to pour out everything to this man. But her head and reason warned her to just concentrate on telling Alan about her life *before* she'd hit the streets, *before* she'd gotten pregnant, *before* she'd given away her son. There wouldn't be any danger in that. Tonight she didn't want to think about danger or regrets. She just wanted to enjoy being with Alan.

The chauffeur drove them around the city, giving them time to relish the champagne and appetizers, giving them time to talk and simply to gaze into each other's eyes.

When he pulled up under the portico of a three-story brick building, Lisa was almost sorry. She'd love to ride around Portland with Alan in the vehicle all night.

"This was a wonderful idea," she told him as he stepped out of the limo and took her hand to help her out.

"I have them once in a while," he joked. "Just wait till we get to stage two."

Producing a pass card, Alan opened the front door to the club. Once inside, he had to use the card again and then touch his thumb to the small square pad. "It recognizes my fingerprint," he explained.

"No doorman needed."

"No one sees who's coming and going this way. Exclusivity is one of the reasons men join. We can escape here and no one need ever know."

"The club is only for men?"

"I understand there are women's clubs, too. If you want the name of one, I'm sure I can find one."

She was certain she wouldn't be able to afford the membership fee.

"Why did you join?" she asked as they walked down a hall with rich dark paneling, thick carpet and portraits of men who had made a difference in the world placed at comfortable intervals.

"I joined because I wanted to be grounded. I knew the area from spending time here when I was in college. One of my friends from school got a job up here, but he was as busy as I was. I could stop in here to watch a game if I didn't want to sit in my hotel room, or I could play pool, or bring a client to dinner. There are racquetball courts downstairs and workout rooms. It had everything I needed to start making myself at home in Portland."

"I never even knew this was here. It's very discreet."

Again she had to wonder if he'd brought her here to *be* discreet. Here, no one noticed who came and went, and that's the way he wanted it.

"So did you make friends here?"

"Not really. I found a few partners for racquetball, but I didn't join looking for community. I think women do that more than men."

He was probably right about that. Besides, Alan had family ties to give him the community he needed. "You and your brother are close, aren't you?"

"We've had a common goal since we were kids— make the Lazy B a success. I think that brought us close. We disagree a lot because we're different. But we're brothers and that's the bottom line."

The more Lisa knew about Alan, the more she liked him. He had strong family ties and he didn't take them for granted. Relationships took work, and he seemed to understand that better than other men she'd met.

Then why hadn't he gotten involved with anyone since his divorce?

Had he been burned too badly? Had he closed his heart to women, except to enjoy them in bed? Or had he simply learned that nothing lasted forever, and he didn't want to be disillusioned a second time? Was that the real problem with their age difference? She still had romantic dreams and he didn't?

Finally they arrived at a closed, mahogany-paneled door. Above it was the brass letter *B*. "There's more than one private dining room," he explained, and then opened the heavy door.

Inside the room, Lisa took a look around and smiled. It was every girl's dream of what Valentine's Day should be. There were heart-shaped grapevine wreaths on the walls, wound with twinkle lights. A gold sconce held at least ten votive candles that flickered romantically. Besides the serving table covered with a gold tablecloth, a table for two beckoned to them. Its white linen covering was pristine; a dozen long-stemmed red roses in a crystal vase scented the air; ivory china with gold trim and gold flatware sparkled on the table.

"This is *so* lovely." She couldn't stop looking around, noticing every detail.

"Not as lovely as you." Alan's voice was husky as he stepped closer to her.

She was torn between feeling like a princess and wondering if this was his standard operating procedure. Maybe he made all of his dates feel like Cinderella.

"What's the matter?" He apparently saw something in her eyes that concerned him.

Feeling self-conscious, she said, "I don't want to spoil the mood."

He took her face between his palms. "If there's something on your mind, I want to know what it is."

Swallowing hard, she asked, "Do you do this for all your dates?"

"Valentine's Day only comes once a year."

"You know what I mean, Alan. I love the limo, this room, feeling like a princess, but I also have to wonder if you've done all this before, at least a hundred times."

When he dropped his hands from her face, she was afraid she'd blown the night. She was afraid she had insulted him and he'd think she was ungrateful.

His mouth tightened and the nerve in his jaw worked, but his tone was more frustrated than angry when he replied, "I did this for *you*...for us. I've never brought a woman to dinner here before. Sure, I've taken dates to expensive restaurants. I've hired limos. But not as often as you think." After a long look and a pause, he added, "And I don't have lines that I pull out of a book when they're convenient."

She reached out and touched his arm. "I'm sorry I asked. I did spoil everything, didn't I?"

He grasped her hand and took it between his. "No, you didn't. But what makes you think you're *not* special enough for a night like this?"

Whoa. A perceptive man. He'd dived to the bottom line without a blink. Her heart hammered and she thought about telling him everything. But she did want tonight. She did want to feel special, even if in her soul she didn't feel she deserved it. "I guess I'm just insecure. I've never been around anyone...like you."

"I'm going to take that as a compliment," he teased, then led her to the table. "I ordered filet mignon and lobster. I figured if you didn't like one, you'd like the other." After he pulled her chair out for her, he waited until she was seated. Then he took the shawl from around her shoulders, his hand brushing her neck. He laid it on a jewel-toned, cut-velvet love seat, set his hat beside it and joined her at the table.

"I like both," she assured him.

He checked his watch. "We have a few minutes before dinner arrives." He nodded to her locket. "Did you get a new chain for that?"

She took the heart between her fingers. "Yes, I did. The jeweler said even if he repaired the old one, it might break again."

With an unreadable expression, he handed her a small box wrapped in gold foil with a white bow. "Let's get something straight right up front. I do *not* give presents to all my dates. But this is Valentine's Day. I wanted to thank you for helping Christina pick out a car and being so nice to her while you were at the Lazy B."

Alan was making the gift easy for her to accept. If he cached it in terms of gratitude, he knew she wouldn't give it back. How could she refuse a thank-you? "I like your daughter. It was easy to be nice to her."

With excitement flushing her cheeks, Lisa took the bow from the box and unwrapped it. Lifting the white lid, she found a pair of fourteen-carat-gold heart earrings inside. "Oh Alan, they're perfect! They match my locket."

"They're as close as I could get."

She took them from the box. "I'm going to put them on." A minute later, she turned her head from one side to the other, then stood and went around the table and gave him a huge hug. "Thank you so much."

"If I stand up and give you a real kiss, the waiter might see something he shouldn't when he brings in dinner."

Leaning away from Alan slightly, Lisa saw the hunger in his eyes. It mirrored her own desire. She knew he wasn't going to push her to sleep with him, but she also knew by the end of this dinner, she had to make up her mind whether she was going to or not.

If Lisa could have prolonged dinner forever, she would have. She knew the evening would be full of indelible memories—the deepening of Alan's blue eyes whenever their gazes locked, the tiny forkfuls of buttery lobster that they fed each other, the sweet, creamy smoothness of the cheesecake on her tongue, the crooked smile on Alan's lips as he watched her, clearly thinking about more kisses to come. Finally, when they'd poured real cream into their coffee, taken a few sips, then clasped hands across the table, she knew the decision she had to make was no decision at all. She wanted tonight. She wanted Alan. She wanted, for a few hours, the opportunity to be a woman with no history, free to give herself, free to love. Was that too much to ask?

Alan laced his fingers with hers and rubbed the inside of her palm with his thumb. Every nerve in her body seemed to dance with the sensation.

"We have a couple of options for the rest of the

evening. We could go dancing at a club. We could drive around in the limo and drink champagne and eat chocolate. We could find a movie we'd like to see…. Or we can go back to my place. Your choice."

She didn't hesitate for an instant. Even if he'd said they could fly to Paris, that wasn't what she wanted tonight. "Let's go to your place."

His voice was deep and husky when he replied, "Sounds good to me."

The ride to Alan's penthouse was silent. He sat close to her, his hand covering hers. The sexual tension between them hummed, but she had the feeling he wasn't kissing her because if he did, they might be shedding their clothes in the limo.

Shedding her clothes. How was she going to handle that? If he saw her tattoos, they'd get into her background, and she didn't want that tonight.

She'd worry about it once they were in his penthouse.

When Ralph greeted them, Alan just nodded his head, put his arm around Lisa's shoulders and guided her to the elevator. He obviously wasn't in a chatty mood, and she knew they both had one thing on their minds.

As soon as the elevator door closed, he drew her into his arms. "Finally, we're alone," he muttered, and kissed her.

She could feel his restraint. She could feel him holding back. She could feel all of the passion ready to explode. She returned his kiss, easing her tongue into his mouth, making him groan.

When the elevator door opened, Alan scooped her

into his arms and carried her down the hallway, his gaze filled with a fire she was ready, able and willing to feel. "The keycard's in my inside jacket pocket. Do you want to pull it out?"

His arms were busy holding her.

Feeling as if she were doing something new, something forbidden, something exciting, she reached inside his jacket and felt the heat of him. The nerve in his jaw twitched and she could tell he was as aroused as she was. She wanted to touch his chest underneath the shirt. She wanted to touch even more.

She found the pocket and then the card. Taking it from his jacket, she murmured, "Everything's high tech now."

"Except for the things that matter."

She knew he meant a man and woman's response to each other, intimate caresses, joining bodies.

As he held her, she pushed the card into the lock. The light turned green. Alan opened the door and carried her inside.

Setting her down, Alan tossed off his hat, shucked out of his jacket, and then he was kissing her—kissing her and holding her and passing his hands up and down her back. She knew he wanted her dress off, but all those little buttons would prevent him from doing it quickly. They hadn't turned the lights on, but twinkles from the cityscape dimly lit the room. If only they could get to the bedroom, if only they could keep the lights off, she could pretend for a while longer. He wouldn't see the tattoos and he wouldn't ask any questions. He'd just make love to her.

Just. She had a feeling making love to Alan was going to change her life.

When he broke away to hold her face and gaze down at her, he asked, "Are you sure this is what you want?"

"I'm absolutely sure. Do you have condoms?"

She hated bringing that up now, but they had to be responsible. She'd bought a pack and put them in her purse.

"I have protection," he assured her. After he kissed her again, he asked, "The floor or the bed?"

She could tell from the tension on his face, the tautness in his arms, that he was holding his desire in check.

"The bed sounds good."

Wrapping an arm around her waist, he kissed her once more and they held the kiss until they reached his bedroom.

Inside, the drapes were drawn. No lights from the city peeked in. It was practically pitch-black. "Can we keep the lights off?" She hoped he wouldn't ask why, hoped he would think she was just shy.

"Sure we can. I can find you by the scent of your perfume. Do you know how crazy that drove me all through dinner?"

She wore a scent that Carrie had given her the first Christmas she'd known her. Lisa was glad Alan liked it. She'd dabbed it at all the appropriate places, and some less appropriate ones.

They undressed each other in a hurry…in as much of a hurry as they could with all those tiny buttons. Alan swore more than once. As soon as he could get her out of the dress, he did. In no time at all, they were lying in his huge bed, forehead to forehead, naked. Then she suddenly *did* feel shy.

He must have sensed that because he whispered, "Touch anywhere you want."

She began with his chest. He began with her breasts. Everything escalated from there.

As Alan kissed her, she gave herself up to his taste, to his desire, to his need and most of all to his hunger. But she didn't only surrender to it, she enthusiastically returned it. Their bodies were soon slick and straining toward each other. When Alan slid his hand between her thighs, she thought she'd come apart.

"I want you." She needed him in that moment.

When he moved away from her, she thought she'd done something wrong. She thought he'd caught a glimpse of her tattoo. She thought—

But then she heard him tearing open a packet and she realized he was using protection. After he'd readied himself, he rose above her, then lowered himself slowly.

She hadn't had sex since she'd gotten pregnant with Timothy and she was tight. It was almost like the first time, only so much better.

Alan stopped pressing into her. "Are you okay?"

"I'm fine. I want this, Alan. I want *you.*"

Her words seemed to break his control. He pushed inside of her swiftly then and she began to feel such wonderful sensations she could hardly breathe. As he thrust in and out, she knew this was an experience she'd never have again. She knew no night could match this one, but she also knew what she was doing with Alan now was a lie...because he didn't really know who she was.

Alan was taking her too high up the mountain to even think about going back. The climb was rapid and steep and intoxicating as her body tensed and her head spun, her limbs tingled, so alive they felt on fire. She clutched Alan's shoulders, willing the moment to never end. But no matter how hard she tried, she couldn't keep herself from flying over the precipice, from shaking. Her orgasm was glorious and absolutely world-rocking.

Alan's groan of release told her he'd found satisfaction, too. All at once, she was exhausted from the emotions, from the evening, from the excitement. When Alan rolled to his side, he took her with him so they stayed joined. They didn't speak. There were no words to describe what they'd just experienced.

Lisa knew Alan felt the same way because he kissed her temple and murmured, "I'm glad you're here tonight."

A few moments later, she heard his breathing become steady and deep, and she nestled into him, letting the afterglow and drowsiness overtake her, too.

Lisa awakened when early light glowed behind the drapes. She vaguely remembered Alan getting out of bed, going into the bathroom, then sliding under the covers again and holding her close. But now she gazed at him in the dim light and realized the shadows weren't going to protect her from what she'd done. She'd made love with Alan under false pretenses, and he was going to hate her for it. He'd see her tattoos as soon as he woke up.

It would have been enough for her to have to explain her past, running away, living on the streets, sleeping in abandoned buildings, letting Craig give her handouts. Maybe Alan could accept all that, along with the tattoos. But she knew Timothy was another matter entirely. Not only the fact that she'd given him away. She knew her bonds with the little boy would be even more difficult to accept. She wasn't his mother anymore, but she was tied to him.

Suddenly she felt altogether panicked and much too vulnerable. She felt insecure and unsure, guilty and regretful, and she couldn't have the conversation she had to have with Alan right now. Not this morning. Not after the night they'd shared. Maybe not ever.

Obviously, she hadn't come to terms with her past. How could she expect anyone else to? She didn't feel worthy of having someone love her.

Taking one last long look at Alan, his tousled blond hair, his firm jaw, his wonderfully broad shoulders, she kept tears at bay and slipped from the bed. Plucking up her underwear, gown and shoes, she tiptoed soundlessly into the living room, where she hurriedly dressed and found her shawl and purse. As she let herself out of Alan's penthouse, she took out her cell phone to call a cab. When she closed the door behind her, she knew she might never see Alan Barrett again.

She couldn't see him again until she was ready to tell him her whole story…and ready to accept him walking away.

Chapter Ten

He was alone. Alan didn't even have to open his eyes to know that.

"Lisa?" he called, hoping she'd gone into the bathroom, or maybe out to the kitchen to make coffee. Yet the hollow emptiness of the whole penthouse told him neither was so. She'd left.

How could she just have gone like that after what had happened last night? They'd been electric from the moment he'd arrived with the limo. They couldn't keep their eyes off of each other. It hadn't been one-sided, and he'd known it as soon as she'd chosen to come back here.

So why had she left without a word? Without a note? Without even a goodbye?

Although he was angry about her leaving that way, he

told himself to back up a step and look at everything…to look at *her*.

She'd wanted to come home with him, he was sure of that. He analyzed everything they'd done after they'd arrived. All of it had been mutual. Still…

He sensed a shyness in her, an innocence that couldn't be faked. As soon as they'd started foreplay, he'd realized she wasn't experienced.

Then the thought hit him square in the gut. Had she been a virgin? Was that possible?

Sure, it was possible. She'd been so tight and he'd just thought…

He *hadn't* thought. That was the whole problem. Oh, yeah, he'd remembered protection, thank God, but he'd been lost in the idea of making love to her. Maybe he hadn't given her enough consideration. She hadn't seemed afraid, but she could have been. He didn't think he'd hurt her. Could a woman hide something like that?

His instincts told him Lisa was hiding a lot more than the pain of having sex for the first time.

Pushing himself up against the headboard, he swore long and hard. When he was with her, he was captivated by her, aroused by her, and his concentration slipped. He protected himself with teasing remarks, and he'd ignored the fact that she might be dancing the same I-don't-want-to-jump-into-this-relationship dance he was. But last night they'd jumped in with both feet.

He could wait and see if she called him, but that wasn't his style. He never waited around for what he wanted, and he wanted Lisa. He wanted to see where this could go.

However, he didn't want to scare her off. Showing up at her apartment or Brian's office could do that. For now he'd be invisible, but he'd let her know his intentions.

A voice inside him whispered, *Just what are your intentions?*

I don't have it all figured out yet.

Feeling foolish, he took the phone book from the nightstand and flipped the pages until he found florists. He was going to send her a bouquet of flowers so big she couldn't ignore them.

When the wonderfully huge bouquet with lilies, roses, tulips and mums arrived, Lisa blinked back tears. And when she took the note from the flowers, her hand trembled as she opened it.

Lisa—Maybe you need some time to absorb what happened between us. I don't. I know I want to see you again. Call me so we can talk about it. You gave me a Valentine's Day to remember, and I hope I did the same for you. We should keep adding to those memories, not let them slip away. Alan

The scent of lilies practically filled the office space. She sank down into her desk chair, staring at the flowers, inhaling their perfume, feeling Alan's arms around her again, his kisses, the intimate touches that had been so sublime.

A member of Brian's sales team who was in the office today—Russ Mahoney, an agent in his late forties who usually didn't have much to say to her—gave her a big grin as he passed her desk. "Somebody spent a bundle to impress you."

She could feel her cheeks heating up, and before she could stop herself, replied, "I don't think he did it to impress me. I think he did it because he cares."

After Russ was gone, Lisa reached out to pick up the phone, yet she couldn't. She couldn't face what she had to tell Alan. His life and hers were so very different— her tattoos were evidence of that. She was afraid she'd be an embarrassment to him. She wasn't even a professional woman in her own right yet.

Putting aside the challenge of revealing her background to Alan, she tried to picture him confiding in his brother that she'd given away a child, telling his ex-wife, explaining to Christina. She could imagine the condemnation she'd see in their eyes. Two people didn't have a relationship in a vacuum. Decisions she and Alan made would affect his family, Carrie, Brian and Timothy. But if she and Alan did get serious about each other, she couldn't go live in Texas. She didn't want to stay that far away. She wanted to see Timothy grow up and share in his experiences. Without her connection to Carrie, Brian and Timothy, she'd be all alone.

Not if Alan loves you.

He hadn't mentioned love. How could he love her already?

You love him.

Yes, she did. But that was *so* different.

She would have to talk to Alan eventually. After all, they were working on the golf resort. But it didn't have to be today, and maybe not even tomorrow. She had to protect herself against the words he'd say, against the deep heartache she'd feel if he walked away from her.

Had being Cinderella for a night been worth this anguish?

Remembering how she'd felt when Alan made love to her, she knew every minute of the night had been worth it. For those hours, she'd felt special. She'd never felt so cherished before.

There were two piles on her desk. One consisted of notes on a new property she had to type up for Brian. The other was the mail that had come in that morning. She pulled the stack of envelopes in front of her, intending to sort through them quickly and get to that report. There were advertisements and invitations as well as bills. She stopped cold when she saw the white, nondescript envelope with her name on it and no return address. It looked the same as the first letter she'd received the day she'd met Alan.

Gauging her level of privacy, she glanced around and saw no one else was around for the moment. Taking her letter opener, Lisa slipped it under the flap and sliced the top edge. Then she pulled out an ordinary piece of white paper.

Typed in the center she read, *"You've got it all now, don't you? You'd better be prepared to share."*

It was obviously a blackmail letter, even though it wasn't demanding money yet. Whoever had written it would demand it the next time, she was sure. Whoever it was had wanted to put a scare into her first. Well, now she was scared, but she *wasn't* stupid.

Reaching for the phone, she picked it up and buzzed Brian.

"Hello." He sounded as if he was distracted by whatever he was doing.

"Brian, it's Lisa. I need to talk to you. Do you have a few minutes?"

Since there was a pause, she knew he was probably busier than he wanted to admit. Yet he told her to come in.

Although Brian motioned for her to sit in the chair in front of his desk when she walked in and said, "Tell me what's on your mind," she didn't do, either. She crossed to his desk and laid the letter on the middle of his blotter. "This is the second one of these I've received. I don't know what to do. I thought you should see it."

After she told him about the first letter, and he'd examined the second, his gaze met hers. "Who do you think could be doing this?"

Now she did lower herself into the chair in front of his desk. "I knew nasty people. You know that. If not somebody I met on the streets, maybe whoever is sending the notes belonged to the black market baby ring."

Brian looked pensive for a moment, then suggested, "Or maybe it's Thad. Do you have any idea where he is or what he's doing now?"

Lisa shook her head. "Absolutely none. He'd wanted nothing to do with me or the baby. He didn't even know I came to Portland until…"

"Until he signed the release forms for the adoption."

"He was headed off for a career in the NFL. If he has that, why would he want to bother me?"

"We don't know what he has. I'm going to call Marian Novak, director of adoption services at the Children's Connection, and set up a meeting. I think Carrie should join us. They most certainly have a lawyer who could tell us how to handle this."

"Do you think we need a lawyer…or the police?"

"No one has made an actual demand yet. If the lawyer at the Children's Connection thinks we should call the police, then we will." Compassion emanated from Brian. "We'll handle this, Lisa. You're not alone."

"Thank you," she murmured, her throat closing tight. She was so grateful to have Brian and Carrie, yet surprisingly the person she wanted to confide in at that moment was Alan.

"You've had quite a morning, haven't you?" Brian asked rhetorically. "I saw that bouquet of flowers. Are they from Alan?"

"I don't want to talk about it right now." Her voice broke.

"Okay. I'll call the Children's Connection. We'll handle this, Lisa, one way or another."

She knew they would, but she was also afraid her past would come rolling out for everyone to see—including Alan Barrett.

* * *

At 3:00 p.m. in the Children's Connection offices, Brian, Carrie and Jillian gazed at Lisa sympathetically.

Marian Novack let the agitated Jillian take the floor. "I couldn't tell you about any of this because it's Children's Connection confidential business. We didn't want a hint of it to get out. A few weeks ago, we were threatened by Timothy's birth father, Thad Preston. He claims he was coerced into giving Timothy up for adoption and said he might file a lawsuit. Jordan Hall, the lawyer we use from Morrison and Treherne, is handling it."

"Hall should handle it really well," Brian muttered. "He charges an arm and a leg." -

"Jordan's definitely in the law business for the money," Marian agreed, "but he's good. The problem is that he's out of town for a few days. We can meet with him as soon as he gets back."

Lisa wondered if Jillian would have told her about all this if she'd only confided in her about the first note. What came first—friendship or Children's Connection business? What came first—love or the way love fit into your life?

"I think we should meet with him," Carrie agreed. "I have to admit, this really scares me. Can you tell us what Mr. Hall thinks about it?"

"Yes, I can," Marian said with a reassuring smile. "We believe Thad's claim of coercion is baseless. Not only do we have Lisa's word that he wanted nothing to do with her and the baby, which I admit could be disputed, but we also have a witness when Thad Preston signed the papers. It was one of his buddies. He told Jordan that Thad couldn't wait to get rid of the responsibility."

"What if his buddy changes his story and backs up what Thad says?" Brian asked.

"Apparently they had some kind of falling out," Jillian explained. "I'm not sure what it was all about, but it had to do with football and the fact that Thad's not playing anymore."

"Not playing? That was his dream," Lisa stated. When she and Thad were dating, he had talked about nothing else. "What if Thad does want to blackmail me? I don't want my past revealed to the whole universe, and I'm sure Brian and Carrie don't, either. I can move away and start over somewhere else, but I don't want to."

Carrie reached over to Lisa and squeezed her hand. "No, we don't want publicity. We'll do everything to avoid it. But if it all comes out, we'll stand beside you."

Lisa blinked fast. "You've already done so much for me."

Carrie looked her straight in the eyes. "You've done so much for us. We have a son because of you, and you're part of our family."

Nothing else Carrie might have said could have warmed Lisa more. Her bonds with this couple and with Timothy would never be broken.

How could Alan ever make a choice to fit into a situation like this? She knew he wouldn't. She wasn't going to call him back.

And the next time she saw him?

They'd be discussing business. Brian would understand if she asked him to pull her off the golf resort project. Right now that was the only solution she could see.

Alan would never understand women.

When he opened the heavy steel door leading into one of the community's fire halls, he replayed his conversation with Brian. Lisa hadn't shown up at a meeting for the golf resort and Alan had questioned why.

Looking uncomfortable, Brian had tried to explain. "She told me she'd rather work on a Hawaiian project, so I transferred her over."

Alan had sworn. He'd been looking forward to seeing her, talking with her, getting everything straightened out. "That's a bunch of hogwash," he'd insisted. "She's avoiding me, and you're helping her."

Brian had looked surprised that Alan had put it on the table like that. "Yeah, maybe I am," he'd said, rubbing his face. "But there's a lot going on in her life right now."

"For instance?" Alan had inquired angrily.

For a brief moment, he'd thought Brian was going to tell him the truth. Instead, his friend and colleague stalled for a few seconds, then gave him a sly smile. "Look. I can't interfere with what's going on between the two of you. But I can tell you this. Lisa's involved in raising money for a teen homeless shelter. There's a dance-a-thon at the fire hall on Saturday night. If you

want to 'run into' her," he'd added almost mischie-
vously, "that might be the place to do it. You'd catch
her off guard and just maybe she'll tell you what's
going on."

Catch her off guard was exactly what Alan was
going to do.

Instead of looking like a fire hall in typical fund-raising
mode, filled with tables holding fried chicken and roast
beef dinners, the entire space had a different atmosphere
tonight. A colored strobe ball dangled from the ceiling.
Couples were dancing. Right now, the DJ was playing
something from the sixties. There was one long table,
where several people seemed to be signing up couples.

Alan spotted Lisa immediately. She was wearing a
long-sleeved, belted jumpsuit in a shade of green that he
knew was the same color as her eyes, as well as the ever-
present locket. Her blond hair caught shimmers of white
light from the peripheral lamps as she attached a number
to a young man's back.

Since, before he cornered Lisa, Alan wanted to know
how the whole thing worked, he spoke to a young couple
just entering the fire hall. They explained they each had
people sponsoring them who were giving a donation for
every half hour they danced. Alan was very glad he'd
brought his checkbook.

Glancing at Lisa, he realized talking to her and
straightening out everything was as important as kissing
her and taking her to bed again. That threw him. Since
when had a woman mattered so much?

Was he just in this for the chase? She'd left him, and so presented a challenge. But after thinking about her the past few days, he'd realized that wasn't it at all. Yes, Lisa Sanders was a challenge, but he liked being with her. In the past, when he'd asked women out, both he and the woman usually figured they'd end up in bed. Yes, that had happened with him and Lisa, too, but they hadn't started out knowing that. And now he didn't know if she'd ever sleep with him again. He remembered the feel of her tucked into his arms. He remembered her nestling against him in the night, her perfume becoming a familiar scent that he reacted to whenever he inhaled it. It was almost like the aroma of cinnamon in home-baked goodies at Christmastime. It evoked sensations he didn't know if he'd ever felt before.

And that was the gist of it. Everything was new with Lisa. He wasn't going to let her run from him without telling him why. He deserved an explanation.

He'd dressed casually tonight in a navy Henley shirt and khakis, and he saw he fit right in. No one was really dressed up, probably because this was more like an athletic competition than a dance.

During his conversation with the couple, he'd noticed Lisa take a seat at the table. Another woman was now attaching the numbers. That suited his purposes just fine.

Crossing to the table, he got in line behind a couple who were registering. They presented their sponsor slips.

He heard Lisa tell them, "After you receive your numbers, give these to the timekeeper over by the stage.

Every half hour you dance, check in with him. He'll make sure you get an official form when you're all through that you can give your sponsors. Thanks so much for coming tonight and helping out."

As Alan heard Lisa's words, he knew they weren't just a pat phrase. She really was grateful the couple had come. Was she so interested in helping teens who didn't have homes because she had had to live somewhere she wasn't welcome?

The couple moved away and Lisa jotted down something on a clipboard in front of her. When she looked up, her expression was priceless. It was a combination of surprise and shock—and maybe even a little bit of joy at seeing him?

"What are you doing here?" she asked, before he could even say hello.

"It's nice to see you again, too." His tone was dry and he wondered just how hard this was going to be.

"You're not wearing your hat. I almost didn't recognize you."

Uh-oh. They were going to have to make small talk. So be it. "You said when I wore my hat, it shadowed my face. I didn't want any shadows tonight."

At that, her shoulders squared and she sat up straighter. "Alan, this isn't the time or place—"

"My phone hasn't been ringing off the hook and my pride kept me from calling you. I agree, we can't have an intimate conversation here." He lowered his voice. "But we *are* going to have one."

She couldn't seem to take her eyes off of him, and he felt the same way about her. Still she protested, "I'm helping with registration and numbering the couples. I can't leave."

"I don't want you to leave. I want you to dance with me. *I'll* be our sponsor. Five hundred dollars a half hour. Can you turn that down when you need donations?"

"You can't be serious."

"I am."

The girl sitting next to Lisa jabbed her with her elbow. "You can't turn down five hundred dollars a half hour."

"Ariel, you don't understand."

"Sure, I do. Even though you haven't told me about him, you have something going on with this guy. It's obvious. So make us some money and dance with him." She gave Lisa a sly grin. "If you don't want to, I could manage to get free for a few hours."

From the conversation, Alan guessed that the two women were friends.

"Thank you, Miss..." He trailed off, waiting for Lisa to fill in.

Chagrined, she made introductions. "Ariel Bridges, meet Alan Barrett, a man who thinks he always has to get his own way."

He didn't bother arguing with her. "Am I going to get my way tonight?"

Lisa looked as if she might refuse, so he added, "All I want to do is dance with you."

Ariel nodded to the dance floor. "Oh, go ahead. The

main rush is over. We're just going to have stragglers coming in now."

The marathon had started at noon to accommodate kids who couldn't drive after curfew.

Alan held out his hand to Lisa. "Let's get our numbers."

He saw conflicting emotions play in her eyes, but then she acquiesced. "Ariel is right. I can't turn down a donation like that."

She could *say* that was why she was going to dance with him, but he knew better.

"Are you and Ariel good friends?"

After a brief hesitation, she replied, "Yes, we are. I've known her since I moved back to Portland. She used to work for Summers Development. She's a paralegal now."

As their numbers were attached to their backs, a fifties ballad began playing. They moved out to the dance floor and Alan took her into his arms, holding her loosely. She was stiff and tense and seemed to expect a confrontation of some sort. He didn't try to pull her too close.

When she saw he wasn't going to pounce on her in any way, shape or form, she said, "Thank you for the flowers. They're beautiful."

"They didn't wilt?"

"No, I took them home with me."

"When I didn't hear from you, I thought they might have ended up in the garbage."

She didn't reply to that gambit. Alan decided he couldn't make small talk for the next half hour, or however long he stayed. "Why did you run off without a goodbye?"

She was silent for a long time as they danced to a song that was sweet and vulnerable and innocent in a way songs weren't now. Finally, she answered him, "I was overwhelmed. What happened between us really shook me up. It was just too big to deal with and it still might be."

"I'm glad I overwhelmed you. I *want* to overwhelm you. In a good way. I never intended to scare you or—"

"I wasn't scared."

He studied her intently.

"I wasn't! You don't scare me, Alan. In fact, just the opposite. What scares me are my feelings."

Was she too young for the relationship he wanted between them? There was only one way to find out. "Spend the day with me tomorrow."

"I can't."

Her answer had come much too fast. "You can't or you don't want to?"

"I'm going to be tied up here until morning and then I have to get a few hours of sleep. Around three I'm going over to Brian and Carrie's to babysit Timothy. I'll be there through the evening." She looked away from Alan, over his shoulder for a few seconds, then her gaze locked to his. "Besides that…" The hesitation was back again.

"Besides that?" He wished she could trust him, depend on him, confide in him.

"I have some things going on in my life that

are…complicated. I'm not sure what will happen next and it's not something I can talk about."

That shut him out, but only if he let it. "Are you involved with another man?"

"No!"

She was so adamant, her green eyes so wide, her expression so shocked that he'd think such a thing, he knew she wasn't. "All right then. If you let me in, if you let me help, maybe everything wouldn't be so complicated. Did you ever think of that?"

"I think about it all the time. But life just isn't that simple, Alan."

"I didn't say life was simple." Now he did pull her a little closer. The pulse at her throat was beating as rapidly as his. So he asked her the question he'd come here tonight to find the answer to. "Do you want me to walk away? Because I'll do that if that's what you want."

As he watched her, her eyes grew shiny and she shook her head. He felt her take a deep breath and he honestly didn't know what she was going to say next.

"How would you feel about coming to Brian and Carrie's tomorrow evening and helping me with Timothy?"

Now he was the one to back up a few steps, figuratively speaking. "I haven't been around kids since Christina was small."

"You don't like children?"

"I haven't really thought about it. I loved Christina, but she was my daughter. I've got to admit I wasn't around much when she was Timothy's age. I've always gotten along with her friends, though. I suppose that should count for something."

Instead of commenting, Lisa just waited.

Spending time with Lisa while they watched a three-year-old wasn't exactly what Alan had had in mind. On the other hand, maybe she'd learn something about him and he'd learn something about her that they wouldn't learn if it were just the two of them spending time together.

"Are you sure Brian and Carrie won't mind if I come over?"

"I don't think they'll mind, but I'll ask them and let you know."

Since the moment he'd seen her tonight, he'd wanted to touch her...wanted to have the *right* to touch her. Now he pushed her hair behind her ear and smiled. "You're wearing the earrings I gave you."

"I'll never forget Valentine's Day," she murmured.

Or Valentine's night, he silently added. When he bent his head to kiss her, she returned the kiss. As the song ended, he didn't care if he emptied his checking account tonight. Dancing with Lisa would be worth every penny.

Chapter Eleven

Timothy, dressed in a red-and-white-striped shirt and navy overalls, perched on Lisa's shoulders as she answered the door. The little boy grinned at Alan. "We're playing horsey. Want to play, too?"

From Alan's expression, Lisa couldn't tell if the idea tempted him to join in or made him want to run in the other direction.

With a chuckle, Alan said, "How about if I come in and we talk about it?"

Lisa tried to glance up at Timothy, who had gone quiet. The idea of discussion was obviously a new concept for him.

"I think we should ask Mr. Barrett to come inside.

We'll take a little break and then have some supper with him," she suggested.

"What's for supper?" Timothy asked.

"Your mom said we should have chicken salad sandwiches and carrot sticks."

"I want pizza."

"Uh-oh." Alan looked amused. "I think you need someone who's skilled in the fine art of negotiation."

"And you're that person?"

"I'm the guy."

Yes, he was the guy—the guy who turned her world upside down, the guy who made her heart race, the guy whose kiss made her dream about happily-ever-after.

Once inside, Alan looked as if he wanted to kiss her. Oh, how she wished he would. But they couldn't do that in front of Timothy.

Alan must have been thinking the same thing because he broke his gaze from hers and bent down to the little boy. "Do you want to play horsey up on my shoulders or down on the ground?"

"On the ground."

Minutes later Lisa laughed as Alan got down on all fours in the living room and Timothy climbed on his back, holding on to his shirt. Alan might have a daughter, but he certainly knew how to roughhouse, and Timothy loved it. Already Lisa knew Alan was a good father—she'd seen him with his daughter. But now she saw how good he could be with smaller children…with her son.

Thoughts of having more kids suddenly sprang to life,

and she wondered what Alan would think about that. Maybe he didn't even want to think about having more kids.

Alan's negotiation skills showed he was an expert in the art of parenthood. He convinced Timothy that they'd order a pizza if he ate chicken salad, too.

After supper, they all played hide-and-seek. It was a big house and Timothy ran from room to room, hiding in what he thought were good places. When Lisa hid, she made sure she was far enough out in the open that Timothy could find her, and Alan did the same. They had him running all over the first floor. Finally, he began to yawn, and his eyelids drooped.

"Read me a story?" he asked Alan.

"Sure, cowboy. You pick one out, and after you get into your pj's and brush your teeth, we'll read it."

Alan gave Lisa a wink as Timothy hurried upstairs.

"You're good at this," she stated.

"You've got to remember, I had some practice."

Meaning, of course, that she hadn't. And she hadn't, really. She'd been away at college. If she told Alan all about it tonight, maybe he'd understand. Maybe he was the type of man who could.

After Alan read him a story, Timothy threw his chubby arms around his neck. "I like you. You come back again."

Lisa could see Alan was touched by the little boy's invitation.

Once they were downstairs, Lisa adjusted the baby monitor in the living room. "There's one in the kitchen, too. Would you like another piece of that lemon cake Carrie left for us?"

"Sounds good."

As soon as they entered the kitchen, Lisa knew everything had changed between them, with Timothy in bed. The buzz was back. The sexual tension raised the temperature in the room. Her nerve endings vibrated with awareness.

"Coffee?" Alan asked, gesturing to the pot, which was still half-full.

Once she nodded, he took two clean mugs from the tree, never removing his gaze from hers. While he poured coffee, she cut the cake. She'd no sooner covered it with the glass holder than he was there beside her. She was still grasping the knife. He ran his finger along the edge, lifting off a fingerful of icing.

"This is the best part," he said, offering it to her.

She opened her mouth, and his finger was on her lower lip, spreading the icing across it. When her tongue slid out to taste it, she found herself drawing his finger between her lips, sucking on it, looking at him with all the feelings that were growing inside of her.

"Lisa," he groaned, not removing his finger, letting the tip of it play over her tongue.

"What?" She knew she was tempting them both.

"I didn't come here tonight to get you into bed again."

"There isn't a bed in sight," she murmured, waiting for his kiss.

He slipped his hands into her hair and tugged her

toward him. The chemistry that had built between them since their first meeting seemed to burst around them. She could have sworn lightning flashed, thunder rolled and the earth shook. Their coming together was that momentous, that hungry, that preordained.

Her fingers went to the snaps on his shirt.

"Don't bother with that," he muttered. "Go for the belt buckle."

She laughed, in as much of a hurry as he was. After all, if she kept her sweater on, he wouldn't see her tattoos. Those tattoos could open the door to absolutely everything else. They'd get to that later.

Alan unsnapped her jeans and pushed them from her hips. With them hanging above her shoes, he pushed her panties down, then lifted her up onto the counter. In seconds, her shoes were on the floor next to her jeans and underwear. Somehow she'd managed to unfasten Alan's belt buckle, but the zipper on his fly was being stubborn and she struggled with it.

Finally he stepped away from her, pulled off his boots, got rid of his jeans and briefs and stood before her, ready, willing and able to make her his. She wanted to be his in all senses of the word.

With his arms circling her, he pulled her to the edge of the counter. She wrapped her legs around him. Seconds later he was inside her, taking her breath away as she grabbed his shoulders and held on. The moment took them away to a place where there was only need and desire and hunger. As he thrust into her, she welcomed him again and again and again, urging him on, saying his name, returning his kisses as he snatched them between thrusts. His world became hers and hers his.

Apparently nearing the end of his control, Alan slid his hand between them and touched her swollen nub, sending her into a million pieces in his arms as he found his release. When she cried his name, he clasped her tightly, pressed his mouth to hers and kissed her so deeply she didn't know where she began and he ended.

They held each other for so many beats of her heart that she knew they belonged together.

Then he suddenly leaned back...leaned away. He looked so serious, she knew she didn't want to hear what he was going to say.

"We didn't use protection. I can't believe I didn't remember." His voice was raw with self-recrimination.

"I didn't, either."

He was studying her as if he didn't quite believe her.

She did some quick calculations. "We should be okay. It's my safe time."

"There *is* no safe time," Alan mumbled as he pulled away from her and took a towel from the counter. "I'll be right back." Snatching up his clothes, he disappeared down the hall to the bathroom.

When Alan returned, Lisa had dressed and freshened their coffee. She offered him a mug. "You drink it black, right?"

With a nod, he took it, stared at it and then set it down on the counter. "If you get pregnant—"

She held up her hand to stop him. "Let's not ask for trouble."

"I think we already have."

"Are you saying what happened was a mistake?"

"The *way* it happened was a mistake. I'm old enough to know better."

"So am I."

The silence that filled the kitchen also weighed down Lisa's heart. This atmosphere wasn't conducive to telling secrets. She wasn't sure what atmosphere was, but the regret in Alan's eyes saddened her. She knew he was remembering another time…when a woman had maybe lied to him about being on the pill…when he'd let passion run away with his good sense. She was remembering, too—the night with Thad when Timothy had been conceived. Both situations seemed the same, yet weren't. She loved Alan. She loved him with all her heart. The idea of being pregnant with his child filled her with joy. Everything for her was different now. She could make a life for herself and a child.

"I'd better be going," Alan said.

"If you stay, we could talk."

"If I stay, we won't just talk. You know that as well as I do."

She wasn't so sure of that. If she told him about Timothy, they'd just be talking.

"I'm going out of town early tomorrow and I haven't packed yet. I haven't even gone through the specs I need to take along."

"Are you flying to Texas?"

"No, Sacramento. When I get back, I'll call you. If I'm tied up for more than a few days, use a pregnancy test. You have my cell phone number, don't you?"

She nodded.

"If you use the test and it's positive, I want to know. Tonight could change the rest of our lives, Lisa. I want you to be prepared for that."

What could she say? That she already knew how life could change in one night? How she wished he'd stay. How she wished she could just ease into all of it. Maybe if she just blurted it out—

Suddenly, she heard the garage door go up. Brian and Carrie were home. She was going to have to wait to talk to Alan, wait to see if she was pregnant, wait for him to return from his business trip.

Life seemed to be just one big wait.

Alan pulled her to him, gave her a sweet, deep kiss and stepped away…just before Brian and Carrie walked in the door.

The following evening, Lisa had just stepped out of the shower when her phone rang. Wrapping herself in a towel, she took another along to dry her hair. When she picked up the phone, she expected to hear Carrie's voice or Jillian's or Ariel's.

Instead, after her hello, a voice murmured, "I wish you were here with me."

Alan. Tears came to her eyes. "I wish *I* was there with you, too."

"Did Brian or Carrie say anything to you after I left last night?"

"Not about us. I think Brian was going to, but Carrie gave him a nudge. They're really trying to stay out of it."

"I imagine that's hard for them."

After a pause, Lisa asked, "What exactly are you doing in Sacramento?"

"Putting together a deal for a Texas client. He wants an orange grove."

She laughed. "You make that sound as if it's something unusual."

He laughed, too. "I suppose it's not. He's always had this dream of someday owning a place in California where he could grow oranges. We all have dreams."

"I dream of you," she said boldly.

"I dream of you, too. That's why I called. I wanted a little reality instead of just a dream."

"I have to ask you something," she ventured.

"Go ahead."

After a pause, as she thought about whether she should ask or not, she decided she'd hesitated often enough with Alan. "Are you really serious about me? I mean, besides the chemistry and all, do you really see me as part of your life?"

When he was silent, she knew she'd put him on the spot. But she wasn't going to turn herself inside out for him. She wasn't going to take the risk of abandonment again unless she knew they had something to build on.

Finally he replied, "I'm serious, Lisa. How about you?"

"I'm serious, too." She'd come to realize Alan was definitely her Prince Charming. She was going to give her heart to him along with her secrets as soon as he returned.

"Then we really have something to talk about when I get back. I should be able to wind this up by Wednesday or Thursday. I'm going to have trouble keeping my mind on work until then."

"Me, too," she agreed.

She wanted to tell him she loved him, but she couldn't do that yet. She couldn't do that until she told him the truth about her life. As soon as he got home, they'd have that talk. As soon as he got home, she'd find out just how unconditional love was…or if he loved her at all.

The smile Lisa carried around with her the next day caused a few raised brows, but she couldn't forget Alan's call or his words.

I'm serious, Lisa.

She knew they had a monumental hurdle to jump over when he got back, but for now she had hope.

She'd just returned from lunch when the receptionist buzzed her.

"A man on two," she said in that polite voice she used when anybody called. "He won't give his name."

"He wouldn't give his name?" If Lisa didn't take the call, chances were whoever it was would simply phone back again.

She picked up the receiver, hoping that Alan just wanted to surprise her. "Hello? This is Lisa Sanders."

"And this is Thad Preston. Remember me?"

For a moment, she froze. Recovering, she managed to reply, "I don't have anything to say to you, Thad."

"Oh, I think you do. After all, I'm the father of your baby."

How much did he know about her life now? How much did he know about Timothy's life? "I signed away my rights and so did you."

"I was coerced."

"That's nonsense. You couldn't wait to sign those papers. You couldn't wait to get rid of me and the idea of a child."

"You weren't around when I signed those papers. You don't know what happened."

Lisa remembered that Jordan Hall had assured Marian Novak he had found a witness who would testify that Thad wasn't coerced. She didn't know if Thad knew that.

"What do you want, Thad?" she asked. "I can't believe you're really interested in—" She was about to say their child's name, but didn't.

"In Timothy? I know his name, Lisa. I know all about him and you and Brian and Carrie Summers. You stayed with them until Timothy was born. They probably even paid your way through college and are maybe even subsidizing you now."

"I'm on my own."

"On your own? I doubt that. Summers even gave you a job."

"I'm earning my place here. I intend to make something of my life."

"And I intend to make something of mine."

"What happened to the NFL?"

"That just didn't work out. Now I have to find something that does. I want fifty thousand dollars from you or I'll go to the press. I'll tell them how I was forced to sign those papers, how you became a slut on the streets begging for food, how you took advantage of a couple, how you're still sponging off of them."

"None of that is true!"

"Oh, it's based on half-truths. That's all I need to get the story published."

"No one would publish—"

"Don't be so sure. News now is different than it used to be. Editors just want to sell papers. I want fifty thousand dollars, Lisa. I'm sure Brian Summers has that in one of his many bank accounts. Just tell him to write out a check."

Lisa's hands were shaking and she knew what she had to do. She had to put a stop to this right now, no matter what happened to her because of her decision. "Thad, I don't have fifty thousand dollars. And I won't go to Brian for it. If you call me again, if you try to extort money again, I'll go to the police." She slammed down the phone.

She was more scared than she'd ever been in her life. She had to tell Brian and Carrie about Thad's threat. She had a feeling he wouldn't go to them. Brian had too much influence, and if Thad knew anything about Brian Summers, he probably knew that. No, he'd come after her, because he thought she was weak. She wasn't weak anymore.

If she had to leave Portland to protect her family, that's what she'd do. Brian and Carrie and Timothy *were* her family. She wouldn't let the rocks Thad wanted to throw at her land anywhere near them.

And what about Alan? a sad little voice asked.

One way or another, she was going to lose him. He wouldn't want to be involved in any of this. His family wouldn't want him to be, either.

Her heart hurt so badly she wanted to sit down in her desk chair and cry. Instead, she squared her shoulders with resolve and headed for Brian's office.

Jillian sat cross-legged on Lisa's sofa the following evening, winding chicken lo mein from her carton onto her fork. She nodded toward the coffee table. "You've got possible job opportunities there from Los Angeles to Vancouver. Are you going to apply to all of them?"

When Lisa had confided everything in Jillian, her friend had offered to pick up takeout and come over to keep her company. Brian and Carrie were adamantly set against her moving away, but she didn't know what else to do. "I've already sent some of them my résumé."

"Do you really want to leave Timothy?"

"I don't have any choice. I don't want Thad's bitterness to get anywhere near him. I don't know what he'll do next."

"You should have called the police."

"Brian took the letters and had a friend who works in an investigative lab dust them for prints. The outside of the envelope, of course, had way too many. But the inside sheet of paper had no unidentified prints on it. No saliva was used on the envelope, either. Thad is smart. I can't prove he threatened me. I can't prove he wants money. It's my word against his."

"So you're going to run."

"No. I'm going to do what I should have done when I graduated from college. I'm going to get a job somewhere on my own and let Brian, Carrie and Timothy be the family they're supposed to be."

"That's not the way they want it."

Lisa set her carton of beef and broccoli on the coffee table, not hungry at all. "Deep down, maybe they do. Carrie has never pushed me away, but maybe she's wanted to. If I had adopted someone's child, I wouldn't want the mother around. It would be a constant fear and pressure."

"I think you're wrong. I think Brian and Carrie look at you as a little sister, and they want you to be in Timothy's life, not *out* of it."

Lisa knew talking wouldn't change any of this. Tears welled up in her eyes and she held up her hand to her friend. "Enough. Can we talk about something else?"

Jillian gestured to Lisa's food on the coffee table. "Yes, if you promise to eat."

With a roll of her eyes, Lisa picked up the carton again. "Let's talk about the Logans. Have you planned another get-together to reunite your father and his brother?"

"Oh, great. You want to talk about *my* family mess."

Lisa managed a small smile. "It will distract me from what's going on with me. Your potluck supper with your cousins went really well." Last month Jillian had brought together most of the Logan cousins and a few friends to try to mend a rift between two factions in the family.

"I've got to admit, it went better than I expected."

"I still can't believe you went up to a complete stranger at a conference, after figuring out he was your cousin, and invited him to move back to Portland to mend a rift in the family."

"Jake's father and my dad haven't spoken for years. They're brothers, for goodness sakes! They were always competitive, but then one thing stacked up on top of the other until there was no communication between them at all."

"It's a shame your dad and your uncle didn't come to the supper, too."

"We have a long way to go before that happens. But I think everyone who came understands that family needs to be united instead of divided. What I'm really glad about—besides the Logan family being on the mend— is that Jake reunited with his first love. Returning to Portland was really necessary for him to find happiness."

"He's lucky," Lisa mused. "I hope he can hold on to it."

They were both silent until Jillian advised her, "You can't leave Portland, Lisa. You know you'll be miserable if you do."

Lisa's doorbell rang and she jumped.

"Are you expecting anyone?" Jillian asked.

"No." She lowered her voice. "You don't think it could be Thad?"

Her friend sat up straight and put her food on the coffee table. "I've got pepper spray in my purse. If he makes one bad move…"

"It might be Craig or Ariel. We'll know as soon as I look through the peephole." Climbing off the sofa and hurrying to the door, she peered out.

It was Alan.

He looked so good, she wanted to cry. She opened the door wide, wanting to dive into his arms, but she knew they had to talk first. She knew tonight could end everything between them…or be the beginning she'd always dreamed of.

Chapter Twelve

Lisa could only gaze into Alan's eyes. She could only wish that what she had to say had been already said. Tonight she couldn't evade or elude or hide. It was time for her to tell Alan *everything*.

Jillian cleared her throat, and Lisa realized she and Alan were standing there, holding hands, looking at each other, as if no one else in the world existed.

Turning toward the sofa, she broke eye contact and took a deep breath. "Alan, this is Jillian Logan, a close friend. Jillian, this is Alan Barrett."

Not only had Jillian stopped eating, but she'd closed her container on the coffee table, picked up her purse and grabbed her jacket. "Nice to meet you, Alan," she said as she approached them. "I was just on my way out."

"You don't have to run off on my account. Lisa wasn't expecting me."

With a knowing glance at her friend, Jillian responded, "Yes, I really do have to go. Perhaps we can get to know each other better another time."

When she gave Lisa a hug, she whispered in her ear, "Go for it."

Lisa knew Jillian meant she should reveal all, that she should hope for the best and keep hold of her dreams. Faced with the reality of what she had to do, she drew a deep breath.

As Jillian left with a wave and an encouraging smile, closing the door behind her, Lisa was ready to take the plunge and start somewhere, anywhere, to get her confession going. But then Alan took her into his arms and kissed her. She kissed him back, giving him everything. She couldn't inhale enough of his woodsy aftershave as her hands burrowed under his suit jacket and she wrapped her arms around him. She couldn't feel enough of his strength. She wanted to rip his clothes off, let him undress her, and make sweet love. It could be the last time. Yet she couldn't deceive him in that way. She couldn't make love and not give him the information he needed to freely love her. Right now, he was living under an illusion and she had to dispel that.

When she tore her lips from his and pulled away, he tried to bring her back. But she held firm and braced her palms on his chest. "Wait."

"Wait?" His eyebrows quirked up sexily and she almost lost her resolve.

"What do you want me to wait for?" he teased. "For you to put on a sexy negligee? I'll tell you right now you can just save yourself the trouble."

He would have kissed her again then, but she evaded his mouth. She evaded his arms.

"You're serious, aren't you?" Now he wasn't looking quite so happy or quite so relaxed, and she could see lines of fatigue around his eyes.

"Let's sit on the sofa," she invited, trying to keep her voice sounding natural, trying not to panic.

His expression changed and she could see him distancing himself.

"Just tell me what you have to say. If you've decided you're *not* serious—"

"No, I *am*. That's not it at all. Please, come sit with me."

Frowning, he followed her to the sofa and lowered himself onto it. When she sat beside him, he leaned toward her. "Tell me what's going on."

Her mouth went dry as she gazed into his very blue eyes. Although she wanted to look away, she knew she couldn't do that. This was about pure honesty, and that's what she had to give him. "I'm not what I seem."

At that opening statement, he actually relaxed, and a small smile turned up his lips. "Believe me, I know you're not a hologram."

"Alan, I'm being serious."

Now he saw that she was. He just waited.

Better to show him than to tell him. Pulling up her sweater sleeves, she presented her tattoos. "I got these when I was staying with Aunt Edna…when I was rebelling."

Taking both of her hands, he turned her arms, first examining her wrist with the peace sign and then her forearm with the upside-down mermaid.

He couldn't keep the amusement from his voice as he suppressed a smile. "I like a woman with a sense of fun and adventure, and a bit of rebelliousness. You've kept these hidden since I've known you. Did you think I wouldn't want to be seen with you if your tattoos were showing?"

"It's not just the tattoos. It's what I did after I got them. I wasn't a virgin the first night we made love, and I think you thought I was."

Still, he didn't get upset. "You're twenty-one, Lisa. I wouldn't expect you to be a virgin. I thought you were because you didn't seem experienced, unless you were faking the shyness and the vulnerability. Were you?"

She could see that idea did upset him. In essence she *had* been faking…even lying. "I wasn't faking what I did or how I felt. I'm not experienced, Alan, not in the way you mean. I've only been with one other man—a boy, really. It was my senior year in high school."

Unclasping her locket from around her neck, she handed it to him. "Open it."

"You still keep a picture of him? What happened to him? Was he in an accident or something?"

She nodded toward the locket. "Open it."

With his thumbnail, Alan popped the small catch and

stared down at the baby picture and the lock of hair, surprise and shock on his face.

"I got pregnant," she told him. "Thad wanted nothing to do with me or the baby. Neither did Aunt Edna. So I ran. I returned to Portland. At first things weren't too bad. I found a job waitressing and I had a room at a boarding-house. But I seemed to get sicker each day of my pregnancy. I think part of the problem was I wasn't eating right. So I couldn't keep the job, and I lost the room. I ended up homeless, on the streets. I met Ariel, who was homeless, too, and we looked out for each other. We mostly stayed in abandoned buildings. The guy I went to lunch with that first day I met you worked at a deli. They throw so much stuff away. When Craig found Ariel and me rummaging one time, he told us we didn't have to do that. He'd make sure we got good food to eat. He often gave us handouts and brought food to the buildings we stayed in, and the homeless shelter. I don't know what we would have done without him."

"You were homeless, with no job, no money and no place to live." Alan was repeating it as if he didn't believe it, as if he was trying to understand it somehow.

"No place to live until I met Carrie. I was eight months pregnant when that happened."

"You told me you met her at the hospital." His tone was even, as if he was trying to keep his cool…as if he was trying not to accuse her of lying to him.

"I met her at the Children's Connection. It's an annex to Portland General. I passed out one day on the streets.

Ariel called an ambulance. A nurse in the emergency room, Nancy Allen—she's Nancy Logan now—called in a social worker from the Children's Connection. I was going to go back to a shelter—that's where Ariel and I had been staying at that point. But Brian and Carrie had applied to be adoptive parents, and the social worker matched me up with them. I didn't know what to expect when I met Carrie, but we kind of hit it off, and she was exactly the mother I'd choose for my child."

The realization of precisely what had happened dawned in Alan's eyes. "Timothy. Timothy is your son!" He looked down at the locket. "This is Timothy."

"Yes. Timothy is…" She corrected herself. "Timothy *was* my son. I went to live with Brian and Carrie, and after he was born, I gave him to them."

"In exchange for an education?" Alan looked appalled.

"Oh, no, nothing like that. I mean, after I lived with Brian and Carrie for a little while, I decided on them as the parents I wanted to give Timothy to. So much happened so fast. At first Brian and I didn't hit it off at all, but then somehow we became like a family. He offered to pay for me to go to college, to get me on my feet for the future. He even gave Ariel a job in his offices."

Taking a deep breath, seeing Alan was trying to make sense of everything she was telling him, Lisa kept going. "After Timothy was born, he was kidnapped from the hospital. We spent a few months not knowing if he was alive or dead. Finally, he was returned to Brian and Carrie. A black market baby ring had tried to take him.

It's a really long story. But during the time he was gone, someone who loved babies cared for him and he was well looked after. I don't think he suffered any trauma from it, thank God, or at least none that we can see."

"None that *we* can see." Alan repeated. "He calls you Lisa. What kind of setup do you have?"

She could hear the remoteness in Alan's voice now. What she suspected was true. He didn't love her unconditionally. He might not really love her at all.

It was time for her to finish the story and face Alan's verdict. "When Timothy was missing, Brian and Carrie and I got even closer. We made flyers. We took phone calls. We cried together. When he was returned, we went back to plan A. I knew I could never sever my ties completely with him, and Carrie and Brian knew it, too. When he's old enough, we'll tell him the truth. But I'm their backup, Alan. If anything ever happened to Carrie and Brian, I'd be responsible for Timothy. Most of the time, I'm okay with being more of a sister than anything else to him. Other times, it hurts. Yet being in his life is better than not being in his life. I can understand if you don't want to see me again. I can understand if this ends everything between us. I think I knew it would, and it's why I put off telling you. I shouldn't have. I'm sorry."

Alan continued to stare at the locket. Finally he handed it back to her. "I need time to think about all this."

Unfortunately, she had a feeling time wasn't going to help at all.

Alan was staring at her, appraising her, searching for

something he couldn't seem to find. "I have one question for you. We had unprotected sex. If you find out you're pregnant again, would you give up this baby, too?"

Deep down inside, Lisa had always known this was a doubt that a man like Alan would have about her. Tears welled in her eyes that she couldn't blink away. "I could *never* give up another child. There are so many days and nights I wish I hadn't given up Timothy."

Although Alan didn't say anything, she could read his expression. She could see the doubts there, the lack of faith. He thought that if she was in a jam again, she'd cut and run. She'd abdicate responsibility. She'd give another baby away. Maybe he wouldn't have had doubts if she'd been honest with him from the beginning. But it was too late for that now. It was too late for *them*.

When Alan shifted away from her, she saw the anguish in his eyes. She gave it one last try. "Try to put yourself in my shoes."

"I *was* in your shoes," he replied gruffly.

She shook her head. "I don't mean about being pregnant. I know you never had any doubts about being a father, but I'm talking about right now...us. I fell for you hard. It happened so fast I hardly even knew what was going on. The minute I realized it, I just wanted— I just wanted a dream. I wanted to love you and have you love me without reality crashing in. But when you called and we talked and you said you were serious, I knew I had to tell you about Timothy."

"Lisa, I can't tell you that it would have made any difference if you'd told me up front. The fact that you gave up your baby... It's just hard for me to get past."

Her pride kept her silent. Her pride kept her strong. Her pride told her she could watch him walk away and she'd still survive.

He said again, "I need some time."

She just nodded.

Then he stood, walked out of her apartment and closed the door behind him. She knew he was never coming back.

Crumpling against the corner of the sofa, she dropped her face into her hands and cried. Her world had shattered around her once again, and somehow she had to figure out how to pick up the pieces.

The ring of the phone awakened Lisa the following morning. She'd been up most of the night, switching on the TV, making herself a cup of tea, eating a few spoonfuls of ice cream. No matter what she did, she couldn't numb herself to what had happened. She couldn't forget the look on Alan's face, the judgment in his voice.

Checking the alarm, she groaned. Who would be calling at 6:30 a.m.? She rubbed her eyes. They felt sandy and rough. She could use a few more hours of sleep. Her alarm hadn't even gone off yet.

Then reality broke over her. Something could be wrong with Timothy! She snatched up the phone.

"Lisa, it's Brian. Are you up?"

"Has something happened to Timothy?"

There were a few interminable moments of silence,

then Brian answered, "No, Timothy's fine. You get the *Portland Gazette,* don't you?"

The *Portland Gazette?* Why was Brian calling to see if she read the newspaper? "Yes, I get it. Why?"

"Bring it in and read it."

Thad's threat echoed in her mind—*I want fifty thousand dollars from you or I'll go to the press.*

Sliding out of bed, she ran to the back door and down the steps. Snatching up the paper, she quickly she unbanded it and carried it back inside, the cordless phone in one hand, the newspaper in the other. Sinking down on the sofa, she stared at the front page disbelievingly. The story took up the bottom half. The headline read *Young Dad Forced to Give Up Baby.*

She heard Brian's voice coming from the phone. In shock, she lifted it to her ear.

"Don't panic," he ordered her.

Don't panic? She began to read.

"Eighteen-year-old Thad Preston never had the chance to be a father. When he discovered his girl-friend, Lisa Sanders, was pregnant, he attempted to make things right. He wanted to marry her, to form a family, raise his child. But Miss Sanders wanted no part of that. She ran away from Seattle, coming here to Portland. Mr. Preston says Miss Sanders had another life in mind. 'She wanted to live with other punk rockers and do her own thing. She didn't want to take care of a baby. She lived in an aban-

doned building until she collapsed and had to be
taken to the hospital. That's when she hooked up
with the Children's Connection. That's when everything went downhill for me.'"

Lisa couldn't believe her eyes as she kept reading, fas-
cinated by the concocted story. Thad claimed he'd been
coerced by the Children's Connection into terminating
his parental rights. He set the blame on Lisa as well as
the Children's Connection, saying they'd colluded to
take his infant from him and give the baby to a wealthy
couple, Brian and Carrie Summers. It insinuated that
Lisa might even have turned tricks on the streets when
she first arrived in Portland.

"Oh...my...gosh!"

In her ear, Brian warned her, "It's just a newspaper
article. It will be yesterday's news tomorrow."

"Not before all of my friends and *your* friends see it.
Not before all our business associates see it. Oh, Brian,
I'm so sorry."

"I want you to listen to me, Lisa. You have nothing to
be sorry for. This isn't your fault. Thad Preston is to
blame...and whoever the editor was on the story. I can't
believe they didn't try to get *your* side of this. You'd
better call Alan and give him a heads-up."

She went still. If she'd harbored even the tiniest kernel
of hope that Alan would understand and eventually come
to tell her they could try to make their relationship work,
this article was a death knell for it.

"Alan isn't going to want to hear from me."

"Why?"

"I told him everything last night...about everything but Thad's blackmail attempts. I told him about Timothy. He...he couldn't accept it. Now there's this publicity, too. He'll believe for sure I'm a horrible person. Oh, Brian."

"I think I should put Carrie on."

Brian obviously thought Lisa was going to fall apart into little pieces. And she just might do that later, but not right now. "I'm fine, Brian. I'm not going to get hysterical. What good would that do?"

"Do you want *me* to call Alan?"

"No. If he comes to you, say what you want."

"I'll tell him the truth."

"I already told him the truth, but I'm not sure he believed me. His family would be absolutely mortified at all this."

"Families stand up for each other."

"Yes, well, I'm not going to be part of his family. I'd never fit in." She felt her throat tightening.

"I called Marian Novak."

"At this time of the morning?"

"We have to keep on top of this, and she didn't seem to mind me phoning her this early when I told her what was in the newspaper. The Children's Connection has had enough problems with scandal. We're going to meet with her at one o'clock this afternoon. Do you want me to pick you up?"

"No. I'll meet you there. It might be better for you if I don't come into the office. It will be a three-ring circus if I do."

"No, Lisa, it won't. The people who work with me know better than to read and believe this kind of garbage. I'm amazed the *Portland Gazette* even published this. Whoever the editor was who put this through should be fired. We'll probably never find out."

"It doesn't really matter, Brian. The damage is done. Firing someone isn't going to change that."

"Are you sure you don't want Carrie to come over?"

"No. I'm going to get dressed and come in to work. But prepare yourself, Brian. Believe it or not, most people *do* believe what they read in the newspaper."

She would just have to brace herself for the ruckus to come. If Brian was willing to stand beside her, she wouldn't let him down. She would put in a good morning's work no matter what anybody said.

She thought again about Alan. Was he reading the newspaper at this moment? Was he thinking that it confirmed everything he believed about her?

When she couldn't swallow past the lump in her throat, she said goodbye to Brian and hung up. As she headed for the shower, she resolved to get Alan out of her head...and out of her heart. But she didn't have a clue how she was going to do that.

Lisa's pulse should have raced as she stared into Jordan Hall's brown eyes outside the conference room door. He was a handsome, high-powered lawyer, and most single women in Portland wanted to date him.

Not her.

He'd directed the meeting that Marian Novak had called and Jillian, Brian, Carrie and Lisa had attended. Now he was reassuring her again, as he'd done in the course of the meeting. "Thad Preston doesn't have a legal leg to stand on. I'm not sure what he's trying to do. You know him better than anyone. Why do you think he went public?"

"At this point, I think he's just plain mad. He couldn't scare me enough to pay him, or to get Brian and Carrie to pay him. So he's simply out for revenge. When we were in school, if anyone crossed him, he made them pay."

"I think we should file for a restraining order against him."

"Do we have grounds?"

"This article proves he harbors ill will toward you. I'll see what I can do."

While they were talking, Robbie Logan and his wife, Nancy, approached Lisa and Jordan. Jillian and Marian had gone off to finish other work, but Brian and Carrie joined them now, too.

After hellos all around, Robbie shook his head sadly. "The Children's Connection can't stand another scandal."

Robbie was head of the day care division of the facility. His story was a complicated one. After being kidnapped when he was a child and being raised by abusive parents, he'd gotten involved in the baby kidnapping ring. But his love for Nancy had turned him around. He'd helped the police find Timothy, and Lisa would be forever grateful for that. After he'd ironed out his own legal dilemmas, the Logans had brought him back into their family fold and he was now instrumental in running the day care center.

"Hopefully, we won't have a scandal over this," Jordan concluded. "If this story doesn't die down on its own in the next couple of days—and I do think it will—I'll insist the paper run a rebuttal article."

"What if they won't do that?" Nancy asked.

"If they won't, I'll see that Lisa's story gets told on the five o'clock news."

"I don't want more publicity about this," Lisa protested.

"Hopefully, the situation won't come to that," Jordan assured her. "If you'd rather stay away from the media, I'm sure Marian will be our spokeswoman. She has public relation skills I only dream about."

Lisa relaxed a bit, and then she thought about Alan. Just how was *he* reacting to all of this?

Did she even want to know?

When Alan picked up the morning newspaper outside the penthouse door, he brought it in and tossed it on the coffee table. He'd been in a bear of a mood ever since he'd listened to Lisa's story last night.

And what a story it was.

She'd given up her baby.

Alan felt torn apart by everything she'd told him. How could she give up a child? Had she simply abdicated responsibility? Or had she done what was best for her baby? Would she really never consider doing it again? Those were all questions he couldn't answer, and until he could, he needed distance from her.

Every time he closed his eyes he saw that picture in the locket. He saw Timothy.

Alan had tossed and turned and punched his pillow most of the night. Maybe a cup of black coffee would help. Maybe ten cups of black coffee would help.

It seemed to take forever for the coffee to perk, but finally it did. He poured himself a mug and took it into the living room, where he sat on the sofa and opened the morning paper.

When he saw the headline—Young Dad Forced to Give Up Baby—he skimmed the article. Lisa's name popped out at him and he sloshed his coffee onto the table. What in the hell was this all about?

He read the story three times, then, disgusted, he tossed the paper down again. His gut was telling him the article had it all wrong. Although Lisa had kept a big part of herself hidden, he knew her. She might have been rebellious. Granted she might have been a runaway. But she had a good heart and values that were a moral compass. There was no way she slept with men to make her way. And she definitely *was* sexually inexperienced. That wasn't denial on his part. It was the truth.

But Thad Preston obviously had an agenda.

Alan went to the bedroom for his Palm Pilot. He had a friend who was a private investigator. It wouldn't take long to get information on Thad Preston. It wouldn't take long to find out what was really going on.

Two hours later, Alan had dressed in jeans and a T-shirt and was pacing his living room. Finally his cell phone rang, and he got the rundown on Preston. After thanking his friend, he called Brian.

Brian's voice was cool. "What can I do for you this morning?"

Apparently Lisa had confided in Brian that he hadn't received her story well. "I got the lowdown on Preston. He was thrown out of the NFL because of drug use. He has little credibility. My guess is he's threatening a lawsuit, hoping the Children's Connection will settle for a nice tidy sum, or *you* will…just to quiet everything down."

"Well, he's wrong. He's not getting any money. The problem is I'm afraid Lisa's going to leave Portland."

"Leave Portland? Leave Timothy?"

"Lisa said she told you everything except…Preston tried to blackmail her."

Alan was quiet for a second. "To be honest, I suspected as much after seeing the paper."

Brian explained about the letters and Preston's call.

Even though Alan was still coming to terms with what Lisa had told him, he felt as if he'd done her some kind of wrong. She'd been dealing with all this and had kept silent. Why hadn't she confided in him?

That was easy enough to figure out. Because he would have reacted as badly as he had last night. Instinctively, she must have known that.

He couldn't keep from asking, "How's Lisa holding up?"

"She's humiliated. She believes everybody will think the worst. She's sure *you* do."

"I don't. I'm just trying to accept that she gave away a child."

"Get past that, Alan," Brian advised, frustration edging his words. "Think about what it cost her to do it…the *emotional* cost. Oh sure, she got to go to college. But each time she returned to Portland, she had to watch Timothy with Carrie. She had to know she could never be his mother. What do you think that did to her?"

Alan really hadn't gotten past her story to the feelings underneath. He was beginning to understand Lisa's loss and her fears about telling him the truth. "I ruined everything between us. I didn't accept her unconditionally, and she'll never forget that."

There was a long pause, and then Brian admitted, "I did the same thing to Carrie. She kept a secret from me…for years." After another hesitation, he continued, "She'd been the victim of a violent crime. When she was still traumatized, her mother coerced her into making a decision she still regrets. Because she believed I could never accept what happened to her or wouldn't want her if I knew about it, she didn't tell me about all of it until after Timothy was kidnapped. I reacted like you did. I needed time to process it, and I walked away. That was the stupidest thing I ever could have done. Fortunately, she forgave me. Women seem to have that gift."

Alan didn't know what to say, but he did know what to do. The private investigator had given him the name of the motel where Preston was staying. "I'm going to take care of this," Alan told Brian.

"Take care of what?"

"Preston."

"You're *not* going to do anything stupid."

"No, not stupid. I'm going to do something smart."

"Alan…"

"Trust me, Brian. Trust me to fix this for Lisa. Trust me to get my thinking straight in my own way."

Finally Brian grumbled, "All right."

When Alan hung up the phone, a plan had already formed in his head. He just had to make a few calls and then he'd be ready to confront Preston, face-to-face.

Chapter Thirteen

Thad Preston let Alan inside his motel room, appearing wary. "You said you want to do another story on me. What paper did you say you're with?"

Ever since he'd read the article, Alan had had to tamp down his anger. He knew it wouldn't get him anywhere. "Yes, I want to do a story…a *true* story."

Thad was dressed in jeans and an oversize T-shirt. His brown hair was standing up all over and he had at least two days worth of beard stubble. He looked as if he needed help, and that's what Alan was here to offer.

"I did tell the truth." The twenty-one-year-old's chin jutted out belligerently.

"No, you didn't, because I know Lisa and I believe her.

You have no credibility, Thad. The NFL kicked you out because of drugs."

"I got injured," he said, seemingly outraged.

"You got injured—a nonserious injury. That happened because you were on drugs. I have the lab sheet." Alan took the faxed paper out of his pocket and waved it. "How about if I call a reporter to do a story on that?"

Thad made a grab for the paper, but Alan pulled it away. "This isn't my only copy. Along with this, there's a witness who was with you when you signed the papers from the Children's Connection and will testify that you were *not* coerced."

"Yeah—Chris. He's a buddy. He'll say whatever I need him to say."

"No, he won't. Apparently you owe him money, and he knows he'll never collect."

"Chris wouldn't sell me out." But Thad suddenly didn't sound so sure.

Alan just let reality sink in. "You've no basis for a lawsuit. You can't even *afford* a lawsuit."

"My parents gave me the retainer."

"And what happens when that runs out? A lawyer won't work for free, especially if he knows he doesn't have a chance to win. You're not going to get a settlement from the Children's Connection, and you're not going to get a settlement from Brian and Carrie Summers."

"How do you know that?"

"Because I'm a friend of theirs, and I gave Brian a copy of *this*."

Looking deflated, but trying to find a bright spot, Thad sank down onto one of the beds. "Maybe if some L.A. director sees me on the news, he'll want to make a movie out of my story."

"You've had your fifteen minutes of fame, Thad. That article is it. A spokesman from the Children's Connection will be interviewed on Channel 6 tonight. Your version of the truth won't stand a chance."

Thad looked worried and lost, as if he had no idea what to do next.

"Do you want to turn your life around?"

He glanced at Alan. "Just how am I going to do that with no money and no job? My parents said they've given me everything they're going to."

"I might be willing to help."

Thad looked hopeful again. "Are you going to pay me to stay away from my kid?"

"No. I'm not. No one is. Even if I paid you, the money would run out. You'd spend it on drugs or booze, and then where would you be?"

"So just how do you want to help?"

Using reason instead of emotion, Alan had considered what would be best for everyone. "I have a plane and a pilot ready to fly you to Arizona, to the best rehab facility in the country, all expenses paid. I also know someone who bought an orange grove in California who needs help renovating the ranch house and with general outside work. You can go there after rehab and prove you can stay clean. If you do that for six months, I have a friend in Sacramento who owns a software company. They design video games. I noticed on your transcript that you're good with computers. A job will be waiting for you there if you get through the rest."

Alan could see Thad running all of it through his head before he asked, "Just why would you do this?"

"Because I think everyone deserves at least one second chance."

Thad looked down at his hands. They were trembling a bit. "I don't have any choice, do I? My folks don't want me back home. My credit cards are maxed out. The manager is going to kick me out of here after tonight."

"You have to want this, Thad. You have to want a future. Otherwise, we're both wasting our time and money."

"I thought my future was over when I got kicked out of the NFL."

"You thought wrong."

Thad stood, went over to the window and stared out at the parking lot. Then he turned around. "When do I leave?"

"Get your gear together and I'll take you to the airport now."

When Thad nodded, Alan breathed a sigh of relief. He also prayed that Lisa believed in second chances, too, because he needed a second chance from her.

When Alan strode into the jewelry store, it was almost 7:00 p.m. He'd spent more time with Thad than he'd intended, driving him to the airport, talking with him some more and keeping his eye on him while the pilot went through the preflight check. Alan had to make sure Thad was serious about rehab, serious about starting over. The twenty-one-year-old had hit bottom and didn't know what else to do. He'd latched on to the lifeline Alan was providing, knowing if he didn't, he'd have no future…at least not one that didn't involve jail or living on the streets. His plane ride to Arizona was a start. There would be a counselor from the facility in Phoenix to meet the plane and take him to the rehab center.

A clerk looked up from her position at the cash register counter and smiled at Alan. He went straight to the glass cases with the engagement rings. Somehow, he was going to win Lisa back. He knew he had preparations to make. He wasn't sure she could ever forgive him, but he was going to do his damnedest to court her and to convince her that he loved her. Because he *did* love her; there was no doubt about it. Brian had helped him see more clearly the monumental sacrifice she had made in giving up her child…because she'd put Timothy first.

At the locked case, one ring stood out immediately. It was a heart-shaped diamond surrounded by smaller diamonds. She seemed to like hearts—her heart locket, the heart-shaped earrings he'd given her. There was a theme here and he was going to go with it.

"Can I see that one?" he asked, pointing to the ring he'd chosen.

It took only a few minutes to get the information he needed—the clarity, carat weight, color and cut of the diamond. With the jeweler's loupe, he studied it and moved it back and forth under the lights. It even looked as if it might be the right ring size.

"A check okay?" he asked.

"As long as you have your driver's license," the clerk assured him.

He'd taken out his license and was writing the check when his cell phone rang. Finishing the check and sliding it across the counter, he answered his phone while the clerk packaged up the diamond ring. It was Christina's cell phone number.

"Hi, honey. What's going on?" He took the bag the clerk handed him.

"Oh, Daddy."

His daughter's voice was full of tears and he began to panic. "Christina? What's wrong?"

"Daddy, it's the car. You're going to be so mad. It's all banged up. The deputy asked if I'd take a Breathalyzer test and I did…." She dissolved into tears again.

A Breathalyzer? His daughter had to take a Breathalyzer test? "Damn it, Christina, I don't care about the car. Are you all right?"

His anger, panic and fear must have upset her more because she didn't answer him, just kept crying. Alan had never felt so helpless in his entire life. "Christina?"

"Mr. Barrett, this is Deputy Moore."

He struggled to keep his voice even. "Is my daughter hurt?"

"No, Mr. Barrett, she is not. She also wasn't drinking,

though the driver of her car was. Both were checked out by paramedics at the scene. The boy was taken to the hospital. The air bag broke his nose. Your daughter didn't want to go to the hospital and since she was seventeen, we brought her here, the Rocky Ridge Sheriff's Office. Apparently she can't reach her mother, though she's been trying. She also could not reach Neal Barrett. He's your brother?"

"That's right. I don't know if she told you or not, but I'm in Portland."

"Yes, sir, I know that, but under these circumstances, I can't just let her go home alone."

"Oh, I understand that perfectly well." Of course, of all days, his plane was on its way back from Arizona. "I'll charter a plane and be there as soon as I can. It might be as late as midnight, though. My guess is she'll get hold of my ex-wife or my brother before that."

"We'll let her keep trying, Mr. Barrett. And if she does need to stay here, I'll make sure I keep an eye on her. From what I can tell, she didn't do anything wrong except have bad taste in boys."

"Can you put her back on the phone?"

"I sure can. Here you go."

"Christina, don't say anything, just listen to me," Alan commanded gently. "I'm flying down. I'll be there as soon as I can. Did you leave messages for your mother and Uncle Neal?"

He heard a small "yes."

"Okay, then just sit tight. One of us will get there eventually. I love you, baby."

"I love you, too, Daddy. I'm so sorry." She began crying again.

"We'll talk when I get home. Hold tight."

He hated to hang up but the sooner he did, the sooner he'd get to her.

The clerk had walked over to the cash register to give him privacy. Now Alan didn't even hesitate to speed dial another number.

"Hello?"

The sound of Lisa's voice made him feel as if he'd come home. He just hoped she wouldn't hang up on him. "Lisa, it's Alan. I have a favor to ask. You have every reason in the world to say no and you probably should, but I'm going to ask anyway. Christina's been in an accident. She's not hurt, but she's at the sheriff's office. I need to fly down there and pick her up and take her home. She can't get hold of Sherri or Neal. In case they can't get to her first, I think she might like having you to talk to. Will you come with me?"

This was a hell of a lot harder than he expected it to be and he wouldn't blame Lisa if she said no.

Instead of answering him, she asked, "Did you see the article in the *Gazette* this morning?"

"Yes, I did, and we have to talk about that, but right now Christina's my main concern. I think you can understand that."

The silence on her end seemed to go on forever. Finally, she said, "I understand. Do you want me to meet you at the airport?"

"No, I'll pick you up. My plane's in use and I have to charter one. I'll make my calls on the way over."

She was quiet again.

"Lisa, thanks for doing this. I'll be there in ten minutes." When he clicked off the phone, he was still worried about his daughter, but he was terrifically pleased that Lisa was going to be by his side.

Lisa wore a headset in the corporate jet that Alan piloted to Rocky Ridge, but they didn't talk much. She knew he was worried about Christina. After all, that's why he'd brought her along. It was hard for her to tell what was going on in his head but she didn't want to distract him while he was flying the aircraft. During the flight, Alan had called the foreman at the Lazy B, who was going to bring Alan's SUV to the airport. He had told Alan that Neal had left that afternoon and wouldn't be back until tomorrow, and that Maude was also away for the weekend.

When they arrived, the SUV was indeed there waiting for them. The keys were under the floor mat.

Tapping his hand on the hood of his SUV, Alan kept his eyes on Lisa's. "I'm going to call Christina's cell to see if she's still at the sheriff's office."

She was.

"Sherri still hasn't shown up," Alan told Lisa. Then he added, "I know she's going to feel guilty when this is all over because she wasn't available."

Lisa knew a bookful about guilt. "Guilt's a terrible emotion. It's so insidious it affects everything."

After a silence filled with a replay of all she'd confessed to him, Alan asked, "Do you still feel guilty because you gave up Timothy?"

"Yes. I probably always will."

Alan fell silent again, and Lisa wished she knew what he was thinking.

As he opened her door for her, their gazes collided once more. That connection she'd felt from the moment she'd met him was still there. Did he feel it, too? If he did, he didn't acknowledge it. He backed away, climbed into the driver's seat and took off for the sheriff's department.

"Was Christina still upset?" Lisa asked.

"It was hard to tell. At least she wasn't still crying."

Five minutes later, they arrived at the Sheriff's department, a one-story brick building, parked in the side lot and went in the heavy glass door. It was just after midnight, but there was a deputy at the front desk and another at one of the three workstations. He stood when they walked in.

"Mr. Barrett? I'm Deputy Moore."

Alan introduced Lisa. "This is my…this is Lisa Sanders. She flew down with me." Alan was already looking around the space. "Where's my daughter?"

"I thought she might like a little privacy. The whole thing was catching up to her. One of the deputies got her something to eat before he went off duty. She's in an office back here that has a couch."

Lisa hurried to keep up with Alan as he followed Deputy Moore down a short hall. The deputy rapped on the door and Christina called, "Come in."

As soon as his daughter saw Alan, she took off the earbuds from her MP3 player and ran to him.

He hugged her and murmured, "It's going to be okay. Everything's going to be fine."

Tears were running down her cheeks as she leaned away slightly. "Not the car," she moaned. "And I have no idea where Mom is. I was supposed to stay overnight at Ginny's tonight."

"Can my daughter leave now?" Alan asked the deputy.

"I just need you to sign a form stating you're her father and she'll be in your care."

Alan nodded.

Christina took Lisa's hand. "Stay here with me, will you? Until Dad signs everything."

"Sure, if that's okay with Deputy Moore."

"Fine with me."

Christina looked miserable as Lisa sat beside her on the old leather sofa.

"Is he beyond mad?" Christina asked.

"He's not talking a whole lot."

Alan's daughter shook her head. "That means he's really upset. I'm going to be grounded for the rest of my life."

Because Christina sounded so woebegone, Lisa joked, "He can't do that. You have to shop for college."

That brought a small smile to the teenager's lips. "I'm so stupid, Lisa. I went to this party with Ginny, one we never should have been at. Our parents thought we were going to the mall, but we knew these really cool guys were supposed to be there. I think I've had a crush on

Colin since I was a freshman. He never gave me a look. Then suddenly tonight, there he was, paying me all this attention, dancing with me. I didn't realize he'd already been drinking before he got there."

"Are you sure you didn't realize it, or did you just not want to see it?"

Christina's face flushed. "I didn't want to see it. Being with him made me feel special. Anyway, he said he heard I got a new car. We went out to look at it and he asked me if he could drive it. I never should have let him."

"But you didn't want to seem uncool. You wanted him to like you. You hoped maybe he'd take you out after tonight."

"Exactly."

When Lisa looked up, Alan was standing in the doorway. Apparently he'd heard some of what Christina was saying. "So he drove your car much too fast. His reaction time was off, he swerved to miss a car turning left, and drove off the road into the base of a billboard. Does that about sum it up?"

"Yes. Daddy, I'm sorry. Nothing like this is ever going to happen again. I promise."

With a scowl, Alan swept off his hat and ran his hand through his hair. "We'll talk about it in the morning. I don't know if the car can be repaired, but if it can, the increase in insurance will come out of whatever you make this summer working at the mall. If it's considered totaled, we'll talk about replacing it with a used one until you can afford to buy a new car on your own."

Christina's eyes were wide, maybe with surprise. Her lower lip quivered. Lisa imagined that Alan had always given her pretty much whatever she wanted. Now he was showing her the consequences of her actions, and that was a good thing.

There was a commotion down the hall and suddenly Sherri was standing there, looking flustered. She hurried to her daughter and hugged her. "Honey, are you okay? The deputy told me what happened."

"Mom, where were you? I couldn't reach you."

"I was with…Russ. I had the cell phone turned off. I'm so sorry. I'll never do that again."

"Don't be silly," Alan said gruffly. "You deserve a life, too. But maybe you *should* check your messages more often."

His ex-wife looked at Lisa. "What's *she* doing here?"

"I asked her to come along because I thought Christina might need her. I didn't know how long you'd be incommunicado."

Sherri didn't look happy about any of it, but that didn't seem to bother Alan. In fact, he stepped close to Lisa and took her hand in his. "Lisa and I will be staying over at the Lazy B tonight."

Ignoring him for the moment, Sherri looked Christina up and down. "Are you sure you're all right?"

"I'm fine. Really."

"I'll call Dr. Cramer tomorrow and make an appointment to check you over."

"All right," Christina agreed. Then she added, "But

tonight, Mom, I'm going to go to the ranch with Dad and Lisa."

Sherri looked dismayed. "Why?"

"Because Dad's been in Portland and I want to talk to him. And tomorrow, he and I have to get things about the car settled. But I'll come home tomorrow night. I know you wanted me to have dinner with you and Russ."

Whether because of guilt from not picking up her messages, acceptance of the situation or a desire to give Christina what she needed right now, Sherri didn't argue.

Alan's hand still enfolded Lisa's. For the first time all evening, she actually felt hope blossoming again. Maybe Alan hadn't dismissed her from his life. Maybe he hadn't asked her along simply to help with his daughter. Then he let go of her hand and she was afraid she was reading too much into that simple hand clasp.

They all walked outside together, and after hugging Christina again, Sherri drove away.

On the ride to the ranch, Alan switched on the radio. Lisa had the feeling he just wanted to give them all a chance to calm down and get back on an even keel. But she knew that wouldn't be easy. He'd almost lost his daughter tonight. In a car accident like that, anything could have happened. She was just so thankful that Christina was unharmed.

At the ranch, they all ambled into the kitchen. Christina asked Alan, "Is there anything you want to know about tonight? I wasn't drinking, Dad, not a drop. I didn't intend *to* drink."

Alan nodded. "That's all I need to hear for now. But I want you to know that when you get to college, you're going to have choices to make. Your mother and I won't be there to give you direction. You can always call us, but for the most part, Christina, you're going to be on your own."

More subdued than usual, she nodded. "I know that now. I mean, I know a wrong choice can be wrong for a lifetime." She gave her dad a hug and then she hugged Lisa, too. "Thank you for coming along to rescue me. We'll talk tomorrow." Stifling a wide yawn, she disappeared into the living room and up the stairs.

Alone with Alan now, Lisa felt jittery. She didn't know what was coming next. She didn't know if a tête-à-tête between the two of them would be good or bad.

He hung his hat on the rack by the door. "I have something to tell you."

"Should I sit down?" she asked lightly, wishing he didn't look so serious.

"It's up to you. I just wanted to tell you I took care of Thad Preston."

Shocked, Lisa just stared at him. "What do you mean, you took care of him?"

"Did you know he was kicked out of the NFL because he was using drugs?"

"No. How did you find that out?"

"A private investigator. After I got the information I needed, I made a few calls. Then I went to see Thad. Fortunately for us, he was ready for some help. My pilot flew him to a rehab facility in Arizona. That's why I didn't have my plane. If he sticks it out and gets clean and stays clean, I arranged for him to work on a ranch in California and then get a position in a software company. But he has to want it."

Lisa's heart was beating so fast she could hardly catch her breath. One word had stood out above all the others. "You said, fortunately for *us,* he was ready for help. *Is* there an us?"

Covering the distance between them, Alan took her hands in his. "Last night…" He stopped then started again. "I was so foolish last night, acting righteous like that, acting as if I had all the answers. I didn't live your life, Lisa. I can only imagine what it was like for you, not having a home, feeling abandoned, being pregnant with no one to care about you or for you."

When tears came to her eyes, she couldn't blink them away fast enough and they fell down her cheeks. "I thought giving up my baby for adoption was the best thing to do for him. I knew Brian and Carrie could give him everything I couldn't. Do I wish now I had made a different decision? Maybe so, but Timothy has a mother and a father whom he loves and who love him. The thing is, Alan, I can't walk away." Her hand went to her locket. "He's part of me. He'll always be part of me. If you can't accept that—"

"I can accept it," he assured her, pulling her closer. "I can accept everything about you, Lisa—from your tattoos, to your spirit of fun, to your career goals. Do you know why?"

"Why?" she asked in a whisper.

"Because I love you. I've been fighting it for all I'm worth. But not anymore." Reaching into his pocket, he brought out a small velvet box.

There was no way she could stem the tears now.

Alan opened the box, took out the most beautiful ring she'd ever seen, and slipped it onto her finger. "A perfect fit, just like us. Will you marry me, Lisa? I promise you, I'll give you all the time you need. You have to be sure that this is what you want, too."

"Oh, Alan, I'm sure." She wrapped her arms around his neck and lifted her lips to his.

Right before he kissed her, he asked, "Is that a yes?"

"Yes," she murmured. Then his lips covered hers.

The long, deep, wet kiss went on and on and on until finally Alan broke away. He scooped her up into his arms. "Will you sleep in my room tonight?"

"With Christina in the house?"

"Christina's going to be in the house during our preparations for the wedding. She's going to be in the house when I want to kiss you. She's going to be in the house whether we're in Portland or in Texas. If it's okay with you, maybe we can divide our time between the two. Isn't it lucky I have a plane that can fly us back and forth?"

He'd meant to make her laugh, but instead she got choked up. "*I'm* the one who's lucky. I never thought I'd find a man to love me for who I am—past, present and future."

Alan smiled. "You found him and he's never going to let you go."

This time their kiss was a sweet promise of everything to come.

Epilogue

In the past ten days, Lisa felt as if she'd won the lottery, taken a trip to the moon and become queen of the universe! Okay, maybe she was exaggerating a little, but not much. As she stood in the ballroom of the Rocky Ridge Country Club, her hand in Alan's, she was so happy she thought she was going to burst.

Christina rushed over from one of the many linen-covered tables. "Your dress is an absolute hit. All the women are talking about it. Even Mom."

A few days ago, when Alan had flown them back to Texas to get ready for their engagement party, Christina had gone shopping with her to choose a dress. It was pink with a western-style bodice, long sleeves and fringed hem.

"Do I want to know what they're saying?" Lisa asked.

Alan wrapped his arm around her waist. "I'm sure they're commenting on how lovely you look. You're beautiful tonight, Lisa. No woman here can hold a candle to you."

Lisa stroked Alan's jaw. "Thank you."

She was thanking him for so much more than the compliments and she could see he understood that. Ever since he'd proposed, he'd made sure she knew exactly how much he loved her. On Sunday evening, when Neal and Maude had returned, he'd called a family meeting to announce their engagement. Sherri and Neal had been astonished. Maude and Christina, who had seen the ring the day before had just looked happy for them. The next day, they'd flown back to Portland to talk with Carrie and Brian.

Brian had looked Alan square in the eyes and said with a smile, "I know you'll take good care of her."

Carrie had added, "I know Lisa will take good care of Alan."

Not only were Brian, Carrie and Timothy here today, but Jillian, Craig and Ariel were, too. Alan had sent his plane back for them. He didn't want anyone important to Lisa to miss this happy celebration.

As Lisa's gaze fell on Timothy, who was rubbing his eyes, she felt a surge of love for him. She and Alan had had several long discussions about him. Alan had insisted he understood the role Lisa would play in her son's life, and that he'd support her one hundred percent. He'd apologized to her again for not accepting her past from the moment she'd told him about it. But she'd understood what a shock her news had been. She'd enjoyed showing Alan over and over that she'd forgiven him.

Now, stepping a little closer to Lisa, Christina said in a low voice, "I know Mom and Uncle Neal were shocked this afternoon when you told us about Timothy. But they came tonight, so I think they'll get used to the idea."

"Of me marrying your dad? Or of me giving up Timothy for adoption?"

"Eventually, both," Christina answered honestly.

The band began to play. To Christina, Alan said, "Honey, if you don't mind, I think I'm going to dance with my fiancée."

His daughter grinned at him. "I don't mind. But I do think I'll talk to the band leader and make sure they play something up-to-date sometime tonight."

Alan laughed as Christina headed for the dais and he guided Lisa to the dance floor. When he drew her into his arms, their guests clapped.

"We've got to set a wedding date," he reminded her. "How about June? Is that enough time for you to be sure you're making the right decision?"

She could tell he was partly teasing and partly serious. "I've made my decision, Alan, when I accepted your ring. I'm sure I want to marry you and build a life with you. In fact, I was a little disappointed when I used the pregnancy test and found out I wasn't expecting. I know you were relieved…."

"I was a little disappointed, too. I didn't make a big deal out of it because I don't want to push you into having children. I know you want to pursue your career."

"I've been thinking about that. Brian already found a replacement for me so I can start working with you. But there's no reason I can't do both, is there? I was thinking I could work part time until our kids are school age, then dig in more. What do you think?"

"Kids?" he asked with a grin. "Like in more than one…"

Suddenly she wondered if she'd read him wrong. "If you only want one…"

Disentangling their hands, he covered her mouth with his index finger. "I was teasing. I know an only child can be a lonely child. Christina has often told me she wishes she had a brother or sister. And I believe if you want to raise kids and work, too, you'll figure out how to do what's best for everyone."

"The more I consider it, I guess I'd want to give my full attention to our baby for at least the first year…maybe two…."

He laughed. "The great thing about being married to me is that I can be flexible! And we don't have to figure it all out this minute. We have until June. Unless you want to try to make a baby before then."

"And shock your family even more?"

"They'll get used to us shocking them." He seemed to think it was inevitable.

Lisa cuddled closer to him as they danced.

When the song ended, he said, "We really should

make the rounds of our guests. There are a few friends I haven't introduced you to yet."

As Alan guided her toward the bar, Sherri approached them.

"Uh-oh," he whispered in Lisa's ear. "I know that look. She has something on her mind."

Sherri gave them both a forced smile, then asked Lisa, "Can we talk for a few minutes?"

Protectively, Alan stepped closer to Lisa. "Why don't you say what you have to say to both of us?"

Lisa patted his arm. "It's okay." She motioned Sherri to an alcove in the back of the room where no one was standing. Then she kissed Alan's cheek. "I won't be long."

Still, Alan looked worried as Lisa followed his ex-wife to the corner of the room.

Once there, Sherri appeared to be…nervous. "I know I haven't been very gracious about you and Alan. After all, everything happened so fast."

"Yes, it did," Lisa agreed, not knowing what to expect. Truth be told, she wanted Alan's family and friends to like her. Yet if they didn't, she was going to love him and make a life with him, anyway.

"Then this afternoon, when you told us about the baby you gave up…"

Lisa tensed.

"I can only imagine how hard it was for you to give up your child. I saw you with Timothy earlier and it's obvious you still care a lot. I just wanted to tell you how I admire the way you stay in his life, yet allow the Summers to be his parents. That's got to tear you up sometimes."

"It does," she admitted, hoping she wouldn't be sorry she had.

To Lisa's surprise, Sherri extended her hand. "I know Christina likes you a lot. And I'm going to warn you, I probably won't be the best ex-wife you'll ever find. Nevertheless, I want to welcome you to the family. Maybe we can learn to be…friends."

In Sherri's eyes, Lisa saw sincerity. She shook her hand. "Thank you."

"Neal will come around. Just give him some time. I think he can already see how happy you make Alan. I know I can."

Apparently unable to restrain himself from watching over Lisa, Alan joined them. "Everything okay?" he asked, looking from one woman to the other.

"We're 'cool' as our daughter would say," Sherri joked. Then she moved away, leaving them alone.

As soon as his ex-wife was out of earshot, Lisa beamed at him. "Everything's wonderful! Sherri welcomed me to the family."

"Only Sherri would have that much nerve," he muttered, shaking his head.

"I'm glad she did. Who knows? We might even become friends."

"That's a disturbing thought," he said dryly. "If you compare notes on me, you'll discover *all* my flaws."

"Flaws? You mean you have flaws?" she teased.

"You know I do," he said, seriously now.

Sliding her arms around him, she responded, "What I know is that I love you. I love everything about you and I always will."

Alan enfolded her in his embrace. "And I love you. For now until…"

"Forever," she breathed.

"Forever," he agreed.

Then he kissed her, and they both forgot they were in the middle of their engagement party.

They were the only two people in the world—a man and a woman who would be in love…who would love each other…for a lifetime.

* * * * *

Look for Jordan Hall's story next month in
MR. HALL TAKES A BRIDE
by Marie Ferrarella
the third installment of the new
Special Edition continuity
LOGAN'S LEGACY REVISITED
On sale March 2007
wherever Silhouette Books are sold.

Happily ever after is just the beginning…

Turn the page for a sneak preview of
A HEARTBEAT AWAY
by
Eleanor Jones

Harlequin Everlasting—Every great love
has a story to tell. ™
A brand-new series from Harlequin Books

Special? A prickle ran down my neck and my heart started to beat in my ears. Was today really special?

"Tuck in," he ordered.

I turned my attention to the feast that he had spread out on the ground. Thick, home-cooked-ham sand-wiches, sausage rolls fresh from the oven and a huge variety of mouthwatering scones and pastries. Hunger pangs took over, and I closed my eyes and bit into soft homemade bread.

When we were finally finished, I lay back against the bluebells with a groan, clutching my stomach.

Daniel laughed. "Your eyes are bigger than your stomach," he told me.

I leaned across to deliver a punch to his arm, but he rolled away, and when my fist met fresh air I collapsed in a fit of giggles before relaxing on my back and staring up into the flawless blue sky. We lay like that for quite a while, Daniel and I, side by side in companionable silence, until he stretched out his hand in an arc that encompassed the whole area.

"Don't you think that this is the most beautiful place in the entire world?"

His voice held a passion that echoed my own feelings, and I rose onto my elbow and picked a buttercup to hide the emotion that clogged my throat.

"Roll over onto your back," I urged, prodding him with my forefinger. He obliged with a broad grin, and I reached across to place the yellow flower beneath his chin.

"Now, let us see if you like butter."

When a yellow light shone on the tanned skin below his jaw, I laughed.

"There...you do."

For an instant our eyes met, and I had the strangest sense that I was drowning in those honey-brown depths. The scent of bluebells engulfed me. A roaring filled my ears, and then, unexpectedly, in one smooth movement Daniel rolled me onto my back and plucked a buttercup of his own.

"And do *you* like butter, Lucy McTavish?" he asked. When he placed the flower against my skin, time stood still.

His long lean body was suspended over mine, pinning me against the grass. Daniel...dear, comfortable, familiar Daniel was suddenly bringing out in me the strangest sensations.

"Do you, Lucy McTavish?" he asked again, his voice low and vibrant.

My eyes flickered toward his, the whisper of a sigh escaped my lips and although a strange lethargy had crept into my limbs, I somehow felt as if all my nerve endings were on fire. He felt it, too—I could see it in his warm brown eyes. And when he lowered his face to mine, it seemed to me the most natural thing in the world.

None of the kisses I had ever experienced could have even begun to prepare me for the feel of Daniel's lips on mine. My entire body floated on a tide of ecstasy that shut out everything but his soft, warm mouth, and I knew that this was what I had been waiting for the whole of my life.

"Oh, Lucy." He pulled away to look into my eyes. "Why haven't we done this before?"

Holding his gaze, I gently touched his cheek, then I curled my fingers through the short thick hair at the base of his skull, overwhelmed by the longing to drown again in the sensations that flooded our bodies. And when his long tanned fingers crept across my tingling skin, I knew I could deny him nothing.

* * * * *

Be sure to look for A HEARTBEAT AWAY,
available February 27, 2007.
And look, too, for
THE DEPTH OF LOVE by Margot Early,
the story of a couple who must learn
that love comes in many guises—and in the end
it's the only thing that counts.

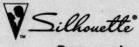

REQUEST YOUR FREE BOOKS!

2 FREE NOVELS PLUS 2 FREE GIFTS!

Silhouette®

SPECIAL EDITION™

Life, Love and Family!

YES! Please send me 2 FREE Silhouette Special Edition® novels and my 2 FREE gifts. After receiving them, if I don't wish to receive any more books, I can return the shipping statement marked "cancel." If I don't cancel, I will receive 6 brand-new novels every month and be billed just $4.24 per book in the U.S., or $4.99 per book in Canada, plus 25¢ shipping and handling per book and applicable taxes, if any*. That's a savings of at least 15% off the cover price! I understand that accepting the 2 free books and gifts places me under no obligation to buy anything. I can always return a shipment and cancel at any time. Even if I never buy another book from Silhouette, the two free books and gifts are mine to keep forever.

235 SDN EEYU   335 SDN EEY6

Name	(PLEASE PRINT)	
Address		Apt.
City	State/Prov.	Zip/Postal Code

Signature (if under 18, a parent or guardian must sign)

Mail to Silhouette Reader Service™:

IN U.S.A.
P.O. Box 1867
Buffalo, NY
14240-1867

IN CANADA
P.O. Box 609
Fort Erie, Ontario
L2A 5X3

Not valid to current Silhouette Special Edition subscribers.

Want to try two free books from another line?
Call 1-800-873-8635 or visit www.morefreebooks.com.

* Terms and prices subject to change without notice. NY residents add applicable sales tax. Canadian residents will be charged applicable provincial taxes and GST. This offer is limited to one order per household. All orders subject to approval. Credit or debit balances in a customer's account(s) may be offset by any other outstanding balance owed by or to the customer. Please allow 4 to 6 weeks for delivery.

SSE06

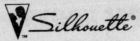
Silhouette®

COMING NEXT MONTH

SPECIAL EDITION

#1813 MR. HALL TAKES A BRIDE—Marie Ferrarella
Logan's Legacy Revisited
Hotshot corporate attorney Jordan Hall had never worried about how the other half lived, until his sister asked him to sub for her at her legal aid clinic. He was touched by his new clients' plight—and by the clinic's steely supercompetent secretary Sarajane Gerrity. Would the charming playboy file a motion to stay…in Sarajane's heart?

#1814 THE BEST CATCH IN TEXAS—Stella Bagwell
Men of the West
Divorced physician's assistant Nicolette Saddler wasn't buying the office buzz about the new doctor from Houston. Then she caught her first glimpse of Dr. Ridge Garroway—good thing he was a cardiologist, because the younger man set her pulse racing! Alas, Ridge suffered the same condition when Nicolette was around. Now to find a cure…

#1815 MEDICINE MAN—Cheryl Reavis
For unhappy divorcée Arley Meehan, the healing began when she met captivating Navajo paratrooper Will Baron at her sister's wedding reception. But would their meddling families keep the couple from commitment?

#1816 FALLING FOR THE HEIRESS—Christine Flynn
The Kendricks of Camelot
Assigned to protect Tess Kendrick and her son, bodyguard Jeff Parker had no sympathy for the spoiled scion of American political royalty who'd ended her marriage on a whim. But when Jeff learned of her true sacrifice to save the family name from her blackmailing ex, he quickly became knight in shining armor to the heiress from Camelot, Virginia.

#1817 ONCE MORE, AT MIDNIGHT—Wendy Warren
Years ago, Lilah Owens had left for L.A. to find fame and fortune after her bad-boy boyfriend Gus Hoffman was busted. Back in town, broke and with a daughter in tow, Lilah was in for a surprise—Gus had gone from ex-con to *engaged* success story. That is, until old passions were reignited—and Gus learned that Lilah's daughter was his….

#1818 ROMANCING THE NANNY—Cindy Kirk
Widower Dan Major was Amy Logan's dream man. But falling for the boss was a no-no for the nanny, since Dan's systematic seduction seemed to be motivated by one thing only—his desire to have a loving stepmother for his daughter. His careful, by-the-book plan wasn't a substitute for true love, and Amy was holding out for exactly that….

SSECNM020